MW01105487

Emma
Bride of Kentucky

American Mail Order Brides Series
Book 15

By Peggy L Henderson

Emma
Bride of Kentucky

Chapter One

Lawrence, Massachusetts, March 1891

Emma Waterston pushed the door shut with more force than necessary. A cold blast of air still managed to rush into the small room of her apartment. A shiver raced down her spine. She rubbed her hands up and down her arms, and pulled her shawl more firmly around herself. The footfalls down the hall outside grew faint.

Alone again after her cousin, Rose Winchester, had left in such a hurry, Emma sighed and moved across the room. She placed another log in the small pot-bellied stove that stood in the corner. It didn't take much to draw out the warmth in the place, especially on a cold March day such as today. She wearily eyed the dwindling pile of firewood. Fuel was costly, and her savings were soon depleted, as much as she hated to admit it.

"Time to sell off a few more gowns," she mumbled. She barely had any decent clothes left.

Her eyes drifted to the front door again. Maybe her cousin had the right idea, after all. Rose was on her way to post a letter to a stranger in Colorado, agreeing to become his wife. Another shiver passed down Emma's spine. Had it really come to this for the both of them? Becoming some man's mail order bride was one of the most detestable thoughts that could ever enter her mind.

Then again, their friends, Gillian and Willow, had gone off to marry men they'd never met before, and both of them seemed happy with their lot in life. Emma rubbed at her arms more vigorously in an effort to dispel the unsettling tingles, as if a man had touched her. Only a

1

destitute woman without any other recourse would even consider such a vile notion, and go off to some unknown part of the country to marry a complete stranger. Why, there was only one thing worse, in her opinion.

You are destitute, Emma Waterston.

Even more destitute than when she'd agreed to apply for work as a seamstress at the textile factory at her friend, Gillian's suggestion. She'd swallowed her pride at the time and accepted the position, as a means to stay off the streets. At least it had been slightly better than taking a job as a scullery maid.

She drew in a deep breath and glanced around the sparsely furnished room of the apartment she shared with her cousin from her mother's side of the family. It was only the two of them now. The financial burden had been slightly easier to bear when Willow and Gillian had still lived with them. Several months had already gone by since the two women had left to begin their new lives, and the money was dwindling quickly.

Anger welled up inside Emma. Less than a year ago, she'd still lived in her mother's expansive Beacon Hills home. She'd had servants, the finest clothes money could buy, and not a care in the world. Suitors lined the front door, hoping for her favors. Now, she was one step away from being homeless and begging in the street.

Emma scoffed. Men. Because of her father, she knew their games too well. She'd flirted with would-be suitors over afternoon tea, had allowed them to take her to social events, even lavish her with gifts, but not one of them sparked even the slightest interest in her. Not that she'd ever planned to marry any of them. They'd only come to call on her because of her wealth, just like her father had only been interested in her mother for her money. When the funds had dried up, so had Emma's callers.

A fire had burned down her place of employment,

and she hadn't been able to secure another suitable position to make ends meet. Not that she'd really been looking. Working for someone as a maid, or cook, or taking care of children was not something she fancied herself doing. The seamstress job in the factory had been bad enough, but it had kept a roof over her head and food in her belly.

The fire at the factory had happened nearly six months ago. Many women had lost their jobs, including Rose, Gillian, and their friend, Willow. Finding work in Lawrence or Boston was hard enough, even without that tragedy. One by one, the ladies had started looking for other means to support themselves, and finding husbands seemed to be one of the most lucrative ways of staying off the street.

Emma's eyes darted to the paper lying on the table. It had fluttered in the breeze created by the open door when Rose left, as if beckoning to her.

The Grooms' Gazette

Rose had been more than eager to show her the paper just a short while ago. Obviously, her cousin was getting desperate, since she was on her way to post a letter in answer to an ad in that paper.

Emma took a slow step toward the table and leaned forward. What harm could there be to just take a quick peek, and see what kind of men advertised for wives? She picked the paper up between her thumb and index finger, as if it was dirty, or the men whose ads populated the page would reach out and touch her.

She shook off the silly notion, took a seat on one of the two bare chairs in the room, and scanned the pages. Her forehead wrinkled as her eyes scrolled down the line of ads.

"Considered handsome by his friends," Emma read out loud, and scoffed. "Most likely he is bald and has a pot belly," she grumbled, and continued to read. "It is desirable that she should have considerable money." This time, she laughed out loud. That sounded like her father, looking for a wealthy woman to take care of him and his habits.

The longer she read, the more dismayed she became. She came across the ad Rose had shown her about the rancher in Colorado. That ad seemed to be the only decent one out of all of them. Disgruntled, she was about to fold the paper and set it aside, when her eye caught the words man of great wealth. She held the paper in front of her face, and her heart sped up.

Man of great wealth, successful Kentucky horse breeder, twenty-six years of age, seeks young lady of good upbringing, possessing social graces and poise, for potential matrimony. Will have the best of everything, and want for nothing.

Emma read the ad several times. It looked too good to be true. Will have the best of everything and want for nothing. Wasn't that the kind of life she'd had before? The kind of life she longed to have again? Her father had taken advantage of her mother's wealth. Past suitors had only been interested when they'd thought she had lots of money. Would it be so bad to consider marriage to someone for the same reasons?

Emma rushed to the desk across the room and pulled open one of the drawers. She removed a sheet of paper and dipped her quill into the ink well. She held the tip to the paper. Her hand trembled slightly, making her writing look worse than it was. Rose should be here to draft the letter. Her penmanship was beautiful.

She'd barely written the first word, when she paused. Yes, she'd ask Rose to write her letter to Mr. David Benton in Kentucky. A beautifully written letter would make a good first impression.

With a satisfied smile, she dipped the quill into the ink again and addressed the letter to her friends and former roommates, instead.

Dearest Willow and Gillian,

I hope this letter finds you well and settled into your new lives. Rose and I are still in Lawrence, and we're managing. Neither one of us has found a new position, yet, and my funds are starting to run low. I've been forced to sell some of my better dresses, and I'm afraid I'll be wearing rags soon, if things do not improve. I believe Rose has followed your example, and has been corresponding with a gentleman in, dare I say it, Colorado. That seems like a world away. I can't imagine travelling so far away, and for what?

I know I've always maintained that I would not consider marriage to anyone except the most affluent suitor, but due to my circumstance, I've been excluded from Boston's better social circles. I hesitate to say, but I'm considering following your leads, and looking for a potential husband through the Grooms' Gazette. In fact, there was an advertisement that looks promising, and I'm considering writing to the gentleman. He is a horse breeder in Kentucky, and sounds rather wealthy. He appears to be just the type of man for whom I am looking.

This brings me to a question I would like to ask, if I may. If you would be so kind and could offer some advice, since you have both become mail order brides, I'd be most appreciative. I must say, the idea is rather distasteful to me, but you both seem to have found happiness. I shall be awaiting your replies most anxiously.

Yours truly,
Emma

Emma copied the letter, then sealed them and addressed one to each of her friends. Willow was now living in Pennsylvania, and Gillian was the wife of a lighthouse keeper in Maine. She shook her head at the idea that she might actually go through with this and write to a man looking for a mail order bride. If he was so affluent, why would he need to send for a wife? Emma dismissed the thought. It didn't matter. This might be her chance to get the life back that she'd been forced to give up after her mother's death.

A gust of wind rattled the windows in the apartment, and rain splattered against the glass. It was getting late, and rushing out into the cold to go to the post office wasn't a pleasant thought. Hopefully the weather would clear by tomorrow.

Emma left the letters on the desk and headed for the small kitchenette to set water on the stove for some tea. By the time the kettle whistled, Rose came barging through the front door.

She pulled her soaked shawl and cloak off, as water dripped from her hair. A bright smile lit up her face.

"Well, I did it. I sent the letter," she announced joyfully. "Hopefully I will hear back soon."

Emma handed her cousin a steaming cup of tea. Rose's smile faded.

"I just worry about you, Emma. What's going to happen when I leave?"

Emma held her mug between her hands and blew at the steam rising from it. She glanced up, meeting her cousin's eyes.

"Well, I thought about what you said earlier, and about Willow and Gillian," she said slowly. "Perhaps you are all correct, and finding a husband through an ad is the right way to go."

Rose raised her eyebrows and her smile returned.

"Let's take a look at the Gazette again. I'm sure we can find someone for you," she said eagerly. Her eyes darted around the room, until they fell on the paper Emma had left on the chair.

"I think I already found someone suitable. I took a look at the ads while you were gone." Emma moved to the desk and set her mug down. She faced Rose. "I was hoping you'd write the letter for me, since you have such beautiful penmanship. You know, to make a good first impression," she added hastily.

"Of course." Rose met her by the desk. She sat and reached for a sheet of paper and the quill. "Who is this man, and what would you like me to say?"

Emma leaned her hip against the desk, then picked up her mug. She took a sip of the hot brew, and stared out the window for a moment.

"Dear Mr. Benton," she dictated. "My name is Emmaline Waterston of Boston, and I happened upon your notice in the Grooms' Gazette, stating that you are in need of a wife. I am twenty-three years old, have lived in Boston all my life, although I currently reside in Lawrence, and come from an outstanding family. I am highly accomplished in running a staffed household, am mild-mannered, and possess impeccable social skills."

She paused, and waited for Rose to catch up with the dictation. "Should I say that I am comely, or not?"

Rose looked up. "You're beautiful, Emma, but maybe leave a little mystery in the letter." She beamed conspiratorially.

Emma nodded and cleared her throat. "I look forward to your response, and hope that you find me suitable to become your wife. Respectfully yours, Emma Waterston."

Chapter Two

Emma accepted the conductor's hand and stepped off the train. She offered him a quick smile and a nod, then scanned the people milling around the train station. She drew in a deep breath. Finally, she'd arrived in Lexington. The five-day trip from Lawrence had been miserably long and exhausting.

A sudden urge overtook her to turn around, climb back on the train, and head home to her familiar Boston, but she curled her toes in her shoes and raised her chin. She'd come this far, and there was nothing left for her in Boston, or in Lawrence. Rose had left the day before she did, and would most likely arrive in Colorado by tomorrow. They'd said their teary-eyed goodbyes on a drizzly morning, each wishing the other luck, and promising to write often.

"It'll all work out," Rose had said, giving her a final hug. "We can both make a fresh start, you'll see."

"I hope you're right." Emma had plastered a smile on her face and waited for Rose to board her train. Her cousin had her own share of troubles, and Emma was ready to leave hers behind. She'd spent her last day in Lawrence packing her two remaining good dresses, cleaning the apartment, and re-reading the letters she'd received from Gillian and Willow.

The advice they'd both given her had been very similar. Both of her friends had found happiness and good husbands. Willow had told her to put her faith and trust in God, that all would work out.

Emma clutched her reticule in one hand and gripped the cloak that was draped around her shoulders. Perspiration beaded her forehead. It was a warm April day, but it was easier wearing it than carrying it along with her traveling bag.

Her stomach twisted into knots as she set her bag on the platform so that she could smooth down the front of her dress, and tuck some loose curls of her upswept hair back under her traveling hat. With trembling hands, she pulled an envelope from her reticule and unfolded the letter it contained.

My dear Emma,

If you find a man half as good as Rhys, then you will find a wealth far beyond that of money. Look what money has wrought in my life. You know I love you dearly, but please search beyond his wealth and be sure you have common values and interests to build a bond of the heart, not the pocket book. I can see your deep frown, my dear friend, and hear your heated response. Know I write these words in love and hope that you will find the happiness and love Rhys and I have secured. Love and friendship always,

Gillian

Emma relaxed the muscles above her eyes. Her friend knew her well, but even though Gillian had found love, and offered advice from her experience, Emma had no wish to build a 'bond of the heart' with a man. Her mother and father had shared nothing in common, at least nothing she'd ever noticed, and money was the only thing that interested him in their relationship. It was all that had kept them together.

Emma laughed. Love had nothing to do with marriage. She would run Mr. Benton's household, entertain guests, and hang from her husband's arm like a dutiful society wife. In turn, she would live in the comfort to which she was accustomed. No more freezing at night because wood and coal were expensive to heat the tiny apartment, or living off of stale bread and cheese because money needed to be saved for rent. No more wearing filthy clothes, doing her own laundry, or sitting in a hot factory all day, sewing garments for the rich. Other women would be sewing her clothes again.

Emma smoothed her gloved hands down the front of her dress, a dark blue traveling gown that had always been one of her favorites. Luckily, she hadn't been forced to sell it, yet. Other than two dresses that would pass for acceptable wear in high society, she didn't own much of elegance.

She'd already thought about what she would tell David - that she'd lost her home and livelihood in a fire. It was stretching the truth a bit, but not by much. There was no need to tell him that she'd been left destitute after her mother's death. She wouldn't even bring up her worthless father.

Mr. David Benton had been vague in his letter to her, but had been eager for her to make the trip to Kentucky so they could meet. He'd even sent her money for a first class train ticket. She certainly wouldn't have had the funds for this journey, even if she had been traveling third class. The last of her money had been spent on the hat and gloves she wore. She had to at least appear as if she still belonged in high society.

Someone bumped her in the side, a man in a hurry to board the train behind her. He offered a quick apology, and rushed for the train. Emma hastily stuffed the letter back in its envelope, then picked up her bag that contained all of her worldly possessions.

She scanned the crowd of people milling about. Ladies in fancy dresses, and men in suits mingled with common people - women in plain garb, and men in work clothes. Her eyes drifted quickly over those people without much interest.

No doubt David Benton would be impeccably dressed, since he was a well-to-do horse breeder. She'd been to the races in New York and Maryland, and it certainly was aptly dubbed 'The Sport of Kings'. People in the horse racing business were rich, and she would soon be among them again. All her worries about finances would be in the past.

In her last correspondence, she'd sent Mr. Benton a description of herself and her travel itinerary, so that he'd know when to come and collect her. He'd described himself as a man in his mid-twenties with dark hair, a moustache, and tall. Of all the men she surveyed, several fit portions of that description, but not the whole package.

Emma paced along the depot. It wouldn't be wise to move too far away from the platform where her train had stopped, in case she'd miss Mr. Benton. The train station in Lexington was quite large, to match this formidable, sprawling city.

Fifteen minutes must have passed and still there was no sight of a man fitting David Benton's description. She blew a quick breath out of her mouth.

"What if he forgot?" she mumbled. "Or got the dates mixed up?"

Emma straightened her back and gripped her bag firmly in her right hand. The wool cloak she wore was becoming unbearably warm in the early afternoon sun. Annoyance at having been left waiting grew. It was time to ask someone about Mr. Benton. She eyed the people going about their business again, then headed for the ticket window.

"Miss Emmaline Waterston," someone called from behind her.

Emma's heart lurched in her chest at the deep voice calling her name. Finally. Curbing her agitation at having been left waiting for so long, she plastered her best smile on her face and swallowed the lump of apprehension in her throat. When she wheeled around, she nearly tripped on a loose wooden board under her feet.

The smile faded and her forehead wrinkled when she glimpsed the man walking toward her. Her eyes darted around to see if it might have been another man calling out her name, rather than the one heading directly at her.

She mentally recited the description David Benton had given of himself - dark-haired, with a moustache, nearly six feet tall, and wealthy. The man in her direct line of vision did not fit that description, not in the slightest.

He was dressed in a simple, light-blue cotton shirt tucked haphazardly inside tan britches that were held up by dark suspenders. The sleeves were rolled up to his elbows, and his wide shoulders did not escape her notice. Neither did this man's dirty blond hair that poked out from beneath a brown cap that reminded her of the newspaper boys back in Lawrence. The other ends of his britches were tucked into old, worn boots.

He stopped just in front of her, and Emma raised her head to look him in the eye. He languidly peeled the cap from his head, revealing a disheveled mop of hair that fell forward over his eyes. His lips curved in a slow grin, creating indents in his cheeks. Emma's heart fluttered inexplicably in her chest. She blinked and shook her head slightly at the reaction. She stared up into deep-blue eyes that threatened to suck her right up. She'd never seen a man this handsome before, even if he appeared unkempt.

"Miss Emmaline Waterston?" he asked again in that rich drawl which she'd already heard once before.

A slight shiver passed down her spine and goose bumps formed on her skin, despite being warm under her cloak.

"Yes," she answered, having to clear her throat to say it a second time. "And you are?"

Surely, this couldn't be David Benton. If so, she'd been deceived.

"Sam Hawley," he said, holding out his hand.

Emma stared at it. She cocked her head to the side, but breathed a sigh of relief when he confirmed that he wasn't Mr. Benton. This man was a mere stable hand, from the way he was dressed.

Reluctantly, she lifted her gloved hand and placed it in his. The warmth and strength in his hand, as his fingers closed around her palm, sent a quick pulse through her that left her momentarily breathless. She pulled her hand out from his and took a step back, shaking off the odd sensation. Her pulse throbbed at her temples.

"I was expecting Mr. David Benton," she murmured, forcing the words from her mouth. "I presume you know him."

Hawley put his cap back on his head before he nodded, then ran a hand along his jaw. "Yeah, I know him. I was told to come and fetch you."

"Fetch me?" Emma's brows rose.

"Benton . . . Mr. Benton couldn't make it," he said, emphasizing the Mr. almost gruffly, as if he'd wanted to say something else. There was a distinct note of annoyance in his tone, like the name left a bad taste in his mouth.

Hawley reached for her bag. Emma gladly handed it over. It was getting rather heavy, and she desperately needed to get out of her cloak.

"Follow me, and we'll get to the farm. It's about a forty minute ride outside of Lexington."

"Very well."

Emma sucked in a deep breath. Her annoyance with David Benton grew. He'd said he'd come and pick her up, yet he hadn't even sent a proper driver. He'd sent a stable hand.

13

What other recourse did she have but to follow this man? She didn't have a penny to her name, and she needed to remain calm in order to make a good impression. If Mr. Benton decided that she wasn't what he'd expected, he might refuse to marry her, and then she'd be in serious trouble.

Peeling her cloak from her shoulders, she followed Hawley as he led the way through the throng of people. He walked briskly, and she had to almost run to keep up with him. If she didn't stay close, she might lose him in the crowd. Emma draped her cloak over her arm and held her hat to her head while trying to keep pace with the man in front of her.

Her agitation shifted from David Benton to his ill-mannered servant. This man had no social manners. He never once glanced back to see if she was still behind him, and seemed to be deliberately walking fast. The look he'd given her when he'd first walked up to her had been almost insolent, as if he detested her.

Emma dismissed the strange feeling. It was silly. Why would a man she didn't know, and who'd never seen her before, have feelings of animosity toward her? Perhaps that was just his character. He'd sounded rude when he'd spoken of Mr. Benton, too. Not exactly a favorable attribute in an employee.

Hawley finally stopped in front of a black, country carriage that stood parked along one of the streets off the main thoroughfare. A team of bay horses stood by patiently. They nickered softly when the man approached, and he gave each of them a pat, then tossed her bag onto the back seat. Only then did he turn to look her way, for the first time since telling her he'd come to take her to David Benton.

Opening the carriage door, he held out his hand to her. Emma stared at it for a moment. Her heart sped up before she even accepted his offer to help her into the rig. She gathered her skirts and set a foot onto the step. The warm hand on her lower back, steadying her, sent an added surge of heat through her, and she nearly fell forward into the carriage.

Hawley closed the door behind her, then stepped up to the rig and draped his forearms over the sides, looking up at her once she was seated.

"Everything all right?" he drawled. "Do you need anything before we get going?"

Emma shook her head to the negative. He offered another heart-stopping grin, his blue eyes trained on her with an intensity that left her heaving for a breath of air, and tipped his finger against the brim of his cap.

Emma clutched her cloak on her lap. He kept his gaze on her for another second, then shoved away and moved to the front of the carriage and swung easily onto the driver's seat. He glanced over his shoulder.

"Make yourself comfortable, Miss Waterston," he called. "And welcome to Kentucky."

Chapter Three

Sam unhitched the team after pulling the carriage into the carriage barn, and led the two geldings to one of the corrals a short distance away. He swiped at some sweat on his forehead with the back of his hand, shoving some of his hair back under the cap. Time to ask old Gus to take the scissors to his mop.

He turned the two coach horses loose in the paddock. A grin formed on his face when they followed their usual ritual of walking off to the middle of the enclosure, then dropping to the ground and rolling in the grass with deep grunts of pleasure. The two geldings were a team in everything they did, not just pulling Mrs. Benton's fine carriage.

Sam glanced toward the big house. Tall-growing junipers and willows partially hid the white columns that framed the front of the mansion, but didn't entirely conceal the large estate. The trees couldn't be tall enough, as far as he was concerned. The Three Elms Farm was his home, and he loved it here, but the big, white mansion was an eyesore, in his opinion. He shook his head and pushed away from the paddock fence.

When had he ever given that house a second glance? He'd never even been near it, except for today, when he'd had no choice but to drive the carriage up to the front entry. He'd only done it as a favor to Gus.

The Benton's long-time general caretaker of the stables and personal driver for Mrs. Benton, Gus Ferguson was like a father-figure to Sam. He'd taken him in and raised him as his own, right alongside his three other sons. Jace, Caleb, and Ben had all left to find work elsewhere.

As much as Sam disliked the owners of the farm, he

couldn't leave. He owed everything to Gus – a home, his job here at the Three Elms Farm, and all his knowledge about horses. Now that Gus was getting on in years, it was Sam's turn to take care of him.

This morning, Gus had barely been able to get out of bed.

"Damn rheumatism," he'd grumbled, limping from his bedroom to the small kitchen, hunched over, and holding a hand to his lower back. Years of working with unruly young horses were taking their toll on him.

"Maybe you oughta stay in bed today. Whatever you need done, I'll take care of it," Sam had offered, handing him a cup of coffee.

Gus had accepted the brew and grimaced when he sat at the table. He'd taken a sip first, then glanced up at Sam, his lips twitching in a smile.

"I don't think I can ask you to do what I gotta do today."

"And I don't think you're in any shape to be juggling harnesses or handling horses today," Sam had countered. "You know you can ask me anything."

Gus had chuckled, which had elicited a coughing spasm. He'd swallowed some more coffee, and peered up at Sam, who'd stood with his hip leaning against the table, waiting for a reply.

"Mrs. Benton needs a ride into Lexington."

Sam cursed under his breath. Of all the things he didn't want to do, spending any time in the company of the farm's owner was at the top of the list. Mrs. Benton was nice enough from what he'd heard, but in all the years he'd been at the farm, he'd never talked to the lady personally. She was one of the rich society women, and anyone who didn't measure up to her standards was looked down upon. That included her employees, especially those who worked in the barns.

17

It had obviously never occurred to the woman that, if it wasn't for the hard working stable hands, she'd have no breeding and racing establishment. She was very good at boasting about her grand horses, and throwing money around, but she'd never gotten her hands dirty in her life. Sam couldn't remember the last time he'd seen her anywhere near the barns. Probably last spring, during the yearling showings, when she'd entertained wealthy buyers.

Sam had mentally scoffed. At least she wasn't as bad as her good-for-nothing son. Once this farm fell into his hands, it would go to ruin faster than anyone could blink.

"Didn't you drive her to Lexington just yesterday?" Sam had asked. It was too late to back out.

"She needs to meet someone at the train station," Gus had said, coughing to clear his throat.

"Another important visitor?" Sam had guessed. "Who's she trying to impress this time? A buyer, or an investor?"

"I've heard it from a reliable source that David's fiancée is comin' in from Massachusetts on the noon train."

Sam's brows had shot up. "Fiancée? Who in their right mind would marry that bas . . . him?"

A twinge of curiosity had coursed through him at the notion that David Benton was engaged. This was the first he'd heard of it, not that he paid much attention to what went on with the owners. It also seemed rather unthinkable, considering David's reputation.

"Heard that he found himself a nice lady, and is ready to settle down."

Sam had scoffed, unable to hide his contempt. "I feel sorry for the woman already. She must be pretty desperate to consider marriage to the likes of him. Is she some horse-faced female who couldn't find a husband in her own social circles?"

Gus had chuckled. "Now, now. Every man can change. Maybe marriage is just what David Benton needs. You never know what effects a good woman can have on a man."

"In Benton's case, I think I know," Sam had grumbled. No woman in her right mind would marry that son-of-a-...

"Best get the team ready," Gus had cut him off. "I sure appreciate you doing this for me. You're a good boy, always looking out for me. You know I'd never ask, but –"

"Get back to bed, you old coot, and you'll feel better in the morning. I'll ask if Millie can come down from the big house and rub some of her special ointment on your sore back and joints."

He'd winked and grinned broadly at the old man. "That oughta make you perk right up."

Sam had snatched his cap from the peg on the wall next to the door and opened it. He owed Gus more than he could ever repay, not that the old man would ever ask for any sort of repayment.

"You need to change your clothes. Mrs. Benton won't be happy, seeing you in your stable duds."

Sam had shot another wide grin over his shoulder. "I said I'd do you a favor, Gus. I didn't say I'd do it in your clothes." He'd raised his hand in farewell and headed up the hill from the caretaker's cottage to the carriage barn to get the team ready to head into Lexington.

An hour later, one of Mrs. Benton's house servants had come to the barn, looking for Gus.

"He's feeling a bit under the weather today," Sam had said. "I can give him the message."

"Mrs. Benton wanted to let him know that she won't be able to go into town today." The young man had glanced around the barn, then stepped closer to Sam and whispered. "There was a lot of yelling upstairs. She and

19

young Mr. Benton had a huge fight again."

Sam had stopped adjusting the crupper around one of the geldings' tails, and looked at the messenger.

"Do they fight a lot?"

The man had sniggered. "Oh, yes, sir. They fight like cats and dogs. Mrs. Benton isn't happy with Mr. Benton at all."

That wasn't too hard to believe, considering she was constantly bailing him out of trouble. David Benton was nothing but a spoiled, rich bully, without regard for anyone but himself. Sam had been on the receiving end of his taunts plenty of times when they'd been younger, and they'd even gotten into a fist fight once, when Sam had stopped him from abusing a horse. Sam had been the one in trouble for it, even though David had beaten him hard enough with a buggy whip that it left welts on his arms and back for days.

There had been other incidents, but he wasn't going to dwell on them. He'd done his best to stay away from David Benton, and do his job and mind his own business. If half the talk going around was true, then David Benton's careless attitude toward anyone had grown worse. His money, or rather, his mother's money, had always kept him out of trouble.

"So, I can unhitch the team?" Sam had asked hopefully. This day might still turn out all right after all.

"No, sir. Mrs. Benton wanted Gus to drive into town by himself, and give his apologies to Miss Waterston for not meeting her at the train station."

"Miss Waterston?" Sam's eyebrows had shot up.

The messenger had handed him a note. "Yes sir. This is a description of the lady, so Gus will recognize her."

Sam scanned the note. Emmaline Waterston. Early twenties . . . dark hair . . . would be wearing a blue dress.

That described a lot of women.

"I'll take care of it," he'd assured the servant, who'd nodded and dashed away.

Sam had finished hitching up the team, then drove the carriage from the barn. He'd stopped to talk to a couple of the handlers who'd been working with some of the two-year-olds.

"Make sure to get Dusty out and let him have a good run in one of the larger pens for a few hours. He's been a bit full of himself lately, and if we want to get any training into him this week, he needs to have his mind on business," he'd called to one of the men. The colt, Diamond in the Dust, was the farm's up and coming racing star, and Sam had high hopes for the two-year-old.

"Where are you going, in that fancy rig?" the man had called back, and several of them whistled good-naturedly.

"Picking up a fancy visitor. Gus is under the weather."

He hadn't wanted to elaborate as to who the visitor was. Rumors spread like wildfire through the stables, and Sam wasn't about to start a new one. If he was, indeed, picking up the future Mrs. David Benton, the entire place would be abuzz about it soon enough.

After parking the rig along one of the side streets close to the train station, Sam had made his way through the hoard of travelers coming and going. He glanced at the paper the messenger had given him, and found his way to the platform when the noon train arrived.

He'd spotted her instantly. A young woman with dark hair swept up under her fancy hat, and in a blue dress. She'd smiled at the conductor who'd helped her off the train, then looked rather lost. Sam had remained rooted to the spot, just studying her. She had to be hot in that wool cloak she wore. She'd looked around, no doubt looking for Mrs. Benton, then pulled an envelope from her reticule and started reading a letter.

He should have walked up to her then, and told her he'd come to take her to the Three Elms Farm, but he hadn't moved. He'd never seen a woman as lovely as this one, and a surge of anger raced through him. He'd tried to wrap his head around the fact that this was David Benton's fiancée. How on earth had someone like her agreed to marry a low-life such as Benton?

Sam had peeled his cap from his head and slapped it against his knee. He'd raked his fingers through his thick mop, then pulled his cap back on. Wasn't it obvious why she'd marry him? Money. Miss Emmaline Waterston looked like a rich lady. The rich tended to stick together and wanted to get even richer. The wealth they had never seemed to be enough for them. She'd fit right in at the Three Elms Farm.

Fifteen or more minutes must have passed, and the lady had looked completely lost, perhaps even scared. She'd started pacing impatiently. When she'd headed toward the ticket window, Sam had made his move. Time to get her to the farm, and himself away from her to clear his head. A woman like that was strictly off limits, and he'd chided himself for even noticing her in the first place.

He hadn't said a word to her on the ride out of town and along the country lane that took them out of Lexington. He'd focused on the rolling green fields, dotted with horses everywhere, rather than the woman sitting quietly in the carriage behind him. Amid the fragrance of spring bluegrass, he'd caught the subtle scent of her perfume every now and then, and he'd put the horses into a fast trot to get back to the farm as quickly as possible.

Chapter Four

Emma's eyes widened at the impressive plantation home that sprawled before her. Once the carriage left the main road, she'd absorbed the beautiful scenery of a long drive down an elm tree-lined country lane. The scene of horses grazing in the pastures on either side of the lane had enthralled her. Several large barns and caretaker cottages had stood off in the distance before the main estate house even came into view. The openness of the land was so different from what she was used to in the city.

Hawley jumped from the driver's seat after the carriage came to a stop. He opened the door and held out his hand. Emma's gaze left the house, her eyes connecting with the blue stare of the man in front of her. The excitement of the grand home drifted away momentarily in those blue eyes. She looked away, fumbling with her cloak.

Hesitating, she placed her hand in his, the strong grip of his fingers sending a surge of awareness through her that was stronger than the one she'd felt nearly an hour ago when he'd helped her into the carriage.

What on earth was coming over her? She should not be acknowledging the driver. Emma quickly stepped from the vehicle and pulled her hand away. Hawley's mouth widened in a slow grin before he reached into the carriage and retrieved her traveling bag.

Emma moved away from him to the front of the vehicle. One of the horses turned its head slightly, even though he was wearing blinkers, and nickered. A smile formed on Emma's lips. How long had it been since she'd been around horses? A surge of anger raced through her. Not since her father sold her beloved Ajax, the horse she'd loved more than anything except her mother.

"Thank you for bringing me all the way out here from the city," Emma said, stepping up to the horse.

The bay gelding sniffed her hand, blowing hot air onto her arm. His teammate craned his neck, looking for attention. Emma laughed softly and patted each horse along its nose. Too bad she couldn't really feel their soft muzzles through her gloves.

"Maybe I'll come visit you sometime, and I'll bring some treats," she whispered.

She raised her head and the smile froze on her face. Sam Hawley stood a few paces off to the side of the carriage, looking at her. Those blue eyes softened considerably from the way he'd looked at her earlier, and he even appeared to be puzzled about something.

"I'm sure someone's expecting you," he said, nodding toward the house. He led the way up the stone steps to the wide portico leading to the front doors. Two massive white pillars graced either side of the front of the home.

Emma gave each horse one final pat, then followed the driver. She lifted her skirt and moved up the stone steps to the door. She nearly tripped from staring upward, admiring the house. This was to be her new home? Butterflies swirled in her belly.

A young maid opened the doors before Hawley had even knocked. The girl looked surprised and a flash of deep admiration passed through her eyes at the sight of him.

"Sam?" she stuttered, and her cheeks turned rosy.

"Just here dropping off this baggage," he said quickly and practically tossed Emma's traveling bag inside the door. He nodded at the maid and turned. His eyes found Emma's and he stared at her for a second. He touched the brim of his cap and all but ran down the steps back to the carriage.

Emma frowned at his rude behavior. His intonation

when he'd said 'baggage' had almost sounded as if he'd been referring to her. She shrugged it off. He was heading back to the stables where he belonged, and she was heading for a new life. She raised her chin and inhaled a deep breath, smoothing the front of her dress with her gloved hand. She stepped inside the home, her shoes clacking on the polished wooden floor.

Her eyes widened and she forced her mouth to remain shut. An impressive winding staircase that led to the upstairs rooms was the centerpiece of the large entry. Emma's belly did a somersault. This house was already grander than her mother's home in Boston. A smile passed over her lips. She'd done the right thing by answering David Benton's ad in the Grooms' Gazette.

"Mrs. Benton is expecting you, Miss," the maid said and curtsied slightly. She smiled shyly, averting her eyes, and stood aside for Emma to fully enter the house.

Emma's brows rose. "Mrs. Benton?" she asked. "I assumed I would be meeting Mr. David Benton."

The maid looked visibly pale for a second. "Yes, Miss," she said timidly. "Mr. Benton isn't home at the moment. Please, come this way."

Emma frowned, but followed the girl through a set of heavy wooden double doors into an impressive drawing room. Who was Mrs. Benton? A slight chill of apprehension slithered down her back. She was in a foreign place, without a penny to her name, meeting a complete stranger she would presumably marry. What did she really know about what she'd gotten herself into?

With a pounding heart, Emma stood inside the formidable room. Large glass doors led to the back veranda, which overlooked fields and fields of pastureland separated by miles of wooden fencing. The white barns looked more impressive than many houses.

"Mrs. Benton will be with you shortly, Miss." The

25

maid curtsied again, and left the room.

Emma took a hesitant step forward. Her hand ran along one of the couches, which was upholstered in ornate flowery fabric, along with the settee and several chairs. A large fireplace dominated one side of the room, while paintings of horses decorated the opposite wall.

The door clicked quietly behind her and Emma spun around.

"Emmaline Waterston."

An older, dark-haired woman swept into the room, her arms extended. She beamed a bright smile and rushed up to embrace Emma like a long-lost friend. Emma stood stiffly in the woman's arms, staving off a sneeze from the strong perfume the lady wore.

"I am so pleased that you're here," she continued in her distinct, southern accent. The woman held her at arm's length and looked her up and down as if she was appraising a newly acquired, expensive purchase. "You didn't say anything in your letter about how absolutely stunning you are, my dear."

Emma's forehead wrinkled. She shook her head slightly and took a step back. "I'm sorry. I wasn't aware that Mr. Benton showed my letter to anyone."

The woman held her fingers to her lips and gasped. "I'm so sorry. How rude of me. I'm Lizette Benton, but you can call me Lizzy. David is my son. And I'm so terribly sorry that David or I couldn't meet you at the train station. Some unexpected . . . business came up, so I sent my driver. I trust him explicitly."

"I understand." Emma choked back a remark about Hawley's rudeness. Perhaps this woman trusted her driver, but how did she put up with his behavior?

Lizette Benton led her to the plush couch. "Sit, my dear. I'm sure you're very tired from your journey. Would you like me to call for some refreshments? Lemonade?

Tea?"

Emma shook her head to decline. It would have been nice for David Benton to have greeted her, rather than his mother, but she swallowed her disappointment. The woman seemed nice enough, and Emma had to make a good impression.

"I have to apologize for my son," Mrs. Benton continued. "He's taken on the responsibility of managing this farm since the death of my husband, rest his soul, and it takes him away from the estate more often than he would like. He should be home later today or tomorrow, and he'll be so pleased when he sees you."

There was an uneasy look about the woman, but Emma had only just met her, so she shouldn't be too quick to draw the wrong conclusion. Something was unsettling about her false smile, however, and the worry that clouded her eyes when she'd said that David would be pleased. Was there something about her appearance that Mrs. Benton thought was lacking? Emma touched a self-conscious hand to her cheek, to sweep back some hair that wasn't there.

"I'll be pleased to meet him, when he gets home." She plastered a smile on her face, then looked around the room. "You have a lovely home, Mrs. Benton."

"Lizzy," the woman corrected her quickly. "I have a feeling you and I will become good friends very quickly." She patted Emma's knee. People in the south seemed much friendlier than the elite in Boston. "We'll have so much fun planning the wedding. A one-month courtship should be sufficient, don't you think?"

Emma blinked. Her heart rate sped up. The reality of what she'd done - coming to Kentucky to marry a complete stranger - was turning into reality. She shook it off. Many couples married by arrangement, and being a mail-order bride wasn't so different from that, was it?

27

"I suppose," she stammered.

From what she'd learned from her friends, a man who sent for a mail order bride married the woman almost immediately. The possibilities of an actual courtship made the idea of having been ordered like someone would order a new piece of furniture, a little less revolting. Even though the thought of marriage was still less than appealing, there was no other alternative. Had she stayed in Lawrence, she would have been out on the street by next week.

Emma's heart sped up. Her life wasn't supposed to have turned out this way. A year ago, she'd been in Boston, content with her life. Then her father had announced that all of their money was lost, that he'd gambled it away on a bad business deal. Shortly after, her mother had fallen ill, and died a few weeks later. Emma's spine stiffened. Her reason for being here in Kentucky was her father's fault. Because of him, she'd lost everything.

Emma glanced out the large windows onto the vast green pastures. She was fortunate to have seen David Benton's ad. For this kind of wealth, she could marry just about anyone. If he was half as nice as his mother, she had nothing to worry about.

Emma smiled at Lizette Benton. "I'm so happy to be here. I hope I'll meet Mr. Benton's expectations."

The woman laughed giddily, which sounded almost as if she were nervous, and patted the top of Emma's hand that she held in her lap.

"David will be very pleased, I'm sure, once he sees you." She cleared her throat and glanced out the window. "I hope you like Kentucky, Emma. We breed some of the finest horses in the country right here in Lexington." There was a distinct note of pride in Lizzy's voice. "Our grass is enriched with limestone, which gives our horses strong bones."

"It's spectacular, from what I've seen so far," Emma said in earnest.

Mrs. Benton smiled. "My grandfather bred horses when he came here from Virginia. The war devastated the breeding industry here in Kentucky, but luckily our farm wasn't affected. We did lose a lot of good stock, but my late husband rebuilt our racing stable, and we're very profitable."

Emma's brows raised. "I thought Kentucky was a southern state." The war between the states was long over, but there was still animosity between the northern and southern states. It had already crossed Emma's mind that she was moving to the south.

Lizzy smiled again. "Kentucky was a border state in the war. We tried to remain neutral, but when push came to shove, many declared loyalty to the Union."

Emma relaxed. At least this was one hurdle that she didn't have to jump in order to be accepted by society in her new home. The question remained if the man who had sent for her would find her appealing.

Mrs. Benton clasped her hands together and stood, as if she'd come to a decision. "You will have to tell me all about your life in Boston, but I'm sure you're very tired from your trip. How about I personally show you to your room, and I'll have Judith draw up a bath for you?"

"That would be lovely." Emma sighed. A bath to soothe her nerves and to relax sounded wonderful.

She followed her future mother-in-law out of the drawing room and up the winding staircase.

"My suite is on the other end of the hall," Lizette chattered, looking over her shoulder. "David's room is the one right here, but I'm not sure when he even slept in it last. He's gone on business so much, and when he is home, he often falls asleep in the study, or the library."

She pointed to one of the doors and continued to head down the corridor. "You'll be in the room at the end of the hall, to give you plenty of privacy."

The woman opened up the double doors at the end of the wide hall in a dramatic fashion and stood aside. Emma's mouth gaped open. She closed it quickly and stepped inside. At first glance, the suite was larger than the two-bedroom apartment she'd lived in and shared with her three friends for nearly a year.

Her traveling bag already sat at the foot of a large four-poster bed. The attractive pink floral covers matched the curtains. The room was furnished with a settee and a dressing table, over which hung an oval mirror in an ornate gold-leafed frame. Large glass-paned doors allowed for plenty of light, and led out to a small balcony overlooking the barns and pastures.

"I hope you'll be comfortable in here."

Emma turned to the woman. She smiled and stepped up to her, bringing her arms around Mrs. Benton's shoulders. She blinked away the tears that threatened to spill.

"This is more than I could have ever imagined, Lizzy. I'm sure I'll be very happy here."

Lizzy Benton returned her smile, although there was that same uneasiness about her as before.

"Well then, I'll leave you to freshen up. Judith will be up shortly with your bath. I'll see you later at supper."

With a nod, Lizette Benton left the room. Emma glanced around. Was this for real? How had she gotten this lucky? She was not going to ruin this chance. Whatever it took, she would impress David Benton. It appeared as if his mother certainly approved of her.

Emma walked to the doors leading to the balcony. She opened them and stepped outside. The air was crisp and smelled of spring. Sweet grass and the fragrance of flowers mixed with the faint odor of horses. It was an intoxicating scent. Her lungs drew in a full breath, unlike the stuffy and stale air she'd been breathing in the city.

Her eyes scanned the fields and settled on the barns. A horse was being led out from one of the structures. The animal appeared fractious, prancing and kicking out its hind legs. When it reared, the breath caught in Emma's throat. The handler looked to be having trouble keeping the animal under control.

Another man moved up to the horse and expertly avoided the flying hooves. He reached for the horse's bridle and seemed to be calming the animal down.

Emma squinted. Was that Hawley? The clothes and the cap looked similar to what the rude driver had worn earlier. Trees obstructed her view when he led the horse along a fence line. Her hand and fingers began to tingle where Hawley had supported her earlier as she'd disembarked from the carriage.

A soft knock on her door announced the maid, and a promise of a soothing bath. Emma abruptly turned away from the balcony and headed back into the room. Time to wash away the grime of five days of travel, along with the unsettling feeling of Hawley's hand on hers, and prepare to meet her future husband.

Chapter Five

Sam held firmly to Dusty's bridle while the unruly colt pranced next to him. An early-morning gray mist hovered over the fields and paddocks, and the breath swirled from the colt's flaring nostrils.

Sam cursed under his breath. He'd had his hands full with another colt yesterday afternoon after he'd returned from Lexington, and this morning Dusty was acting up.

"Ease up on the reins, Ollie. The more you fight him, the more he's gonna fight back."

"I put him out in the pasture yesterday like you said, Sam," the rider called to him from atop the chestnut colt's back. He did as he was instructed and loosened the reins, but the colt continued to shake his head and fight the restraint Sam had on him.

"Then why is he acting this way?"

Sam gritted his teeth. The colt was feeding off his body language, but he couldn't let him loose, not until they reached the training track up ahead. The horse had a lot of pent-up energy, and the run would do him good.

Maybe you should join him and run a lap or two around the oval.

Sam inhaled a deep breath to try and relax, but his tense muscles had already communicated to the young thoroughbred that something wasn't right. Horses were extremely perceptive animals when it came to reading body language, even if it wasn't obvious.

Sam hadn't been able to relax fully since his return from Lexington yesterday afternoon. No, since the moment he'd first glimpsed Miss Emmaline Waterston. She'd been a vision of beauty at the train station, but he'd easily shrugged it off. Until he'd watched the way the carriage team had responded to her, and heard her softly spoken words to the geldings.

32

A haunted sadness had passed through her eyes, but she looked genuinely happy to be near the horses.

"Lonnie told me to put him back in his stall after I turned him out. He said he didn't want the horse to get injured from being loose."

Sam glared up at the rider and visions of the lovely lady from Boston vanished momentarily. Renewed tension poured into him. Lonnie Clayton, the farm's head trainer, had given Sam the responsibility of training the young stock, but he'd been meddling more and more lately.

"I wish he'd mind his own business and let me train these colts without constantly interfering," Sam grumbled loud enough to be heard.

Ollie nodded. "He said the big boss wanted this horse ready to run in Louisville in a couple of months, and not to take any chances."

Sam shook his head. "He's crazy. He knows this horse isn't ready to run a race yet. It's too early in the season."

"We all know that, and I told Lonnie the same thing, but he wouldn't listen."

"I'll talk to him," Sam grumbled.

Not that it would do much good. Lonnie Clayton was the head trainer, and Sam had to answer to him. Although Lonnie had often told Sam that he had a real knack with the young horses, he still called the shots, and they didn't always agree on their training methods.

His grip on Dusty's bridle eased for a split second and the colt took immediate advantage. He jerked his head up and struck out with one of his front hooves, catching Sam in the shoulder. Sam cursed as pain seared down his arm.

"Are you all right?" Ollie called.

"Yeah, I'll be fine." Sam gritted his teeth and renewed

his hold on the bridle. He led the colt onto the training track.

"He's all yours," he called to the rider. "Take him around once at an easy lope. Try and get him to settle down. Then you can open him up and let him run for another lap. Let's see what he's got."

Sam rubbed his throbbing shoulder when the horse cantered off. The colt bucked and shook his head in protest to his rider's hold on the reins. He was eager to run. There would be no sensible training session today. The colt would have been more relaxed had he been granted some freedom yesterday, rather than being boxed up in a stall.

Sam frowned. Lonnie Clayton wouldn't have meddled unless David Benton had said something to him. If Benton was going to make it a habit of telling the trainers how to do their job, Sam might as well find work elsewhere. They would never see eye to eye on anything, least of all how to properly train a horse. His eyes went from the rambunctious two-year-old running down the field to the big house in the distance.

He shook his head. His mind wasn't on the horses this morning. It was up at that house, and on the woman he'd delivered there yesterday. He hadn't been able to get her out of his mind well into the previous night, or all afternoon. The more he'd tried to wipe her from his memory, the more she took up residence there. Perhaps a good kick from the horse was what he'd needed to stop the absurd thoughts in his head. He didn't fraternize with the elite.

He'd only half-listened to Gus rambling on about how the salve Millie had rubbed on him had done wonders for his aches and pains. Everyone knew that Gus, even in his old age, and the estate's curvaceous cook were sweet on each other, even if they both denied it with a

34

vengeance.

The two of them needed to get it out in the open and tie the knot. Why they both fought the inevitable was a mystery to Sam. Gus might claim he was too old for such foolishness, but the spark of infatuation still shone in his eyes whenever he saw Millie. The cook often found an excuse to come visit the barns and drop off special meals with the pretense that they were leftovers and would only go to waste otherwise.

Once he'd covered the second lap around the half-mile oval, Ollie eased Dusty into a trot. The colt didn't look nearly ready to settle down completely, but he'd worked off some of his exuberance during that run. His nostrils flared and both sides of his neck were lathered with nervous sweat. If he could be trained to control that energy, he'd be unstoppable.

Sam rubbed at his shoulder, which throbbed more as the minutes passed. If Lonnie hadn't interfered and had allowed the colt some freedom yesterday, this probably wouldn't have happened.

"Cool him out, then turn him loose in the paddock," Sam called to the rider. Ollie shot him a quizzical look.

"I don't care what Lonnie says." Sam said before Ollie could respond. "This horse needs his freedom, otherwise we'll always have a fight on our hands, and he'll never have his mind on running straight."

Ollie shook his head. "Sure thing, Sam. You're the boss."

Not really, but he'd sure give the real boss a piece of his mind.

Sam headed for the barn. At least the pain in his arm made him forget Miss Waterston for a moment, but only for a moment. He glanced toward the house again. She'd acted all haughty and stiff yesterday, turning her little nose up at him, but her demeanor had completely transformed when she stood petting the coach horses. A vulnerable side had emerged, and besides tenderness and joy, there had also been fear and uncertainty in her eyes. She had no idea what she was in for if she married David Benton.

Gus glanced up from his work when Sam sauntered into the carriage barn. The old caretaker took great pride in keeping each piece of harness well-oiled and all the brass fittings polished until they sparkled like fine jewelery.

"What's got you looking like a mule with its tail caught between the fence gate?" Gus set the leather aside and leaned his palms on his knees.

"Lonnie's interfering with my training," Sam grumbled, still holding his aching shoulder. Gus pointed at it.

"You get into a fight with him?"

"Not yet, but I might." He sat beside Gus on the bale of straw. "Dusty got me with his hoof."

Gus stood and faced Sam. "Let's take a look." He motioned with his fingers for Sam to unbutton his shirt.

Sam frowned, but pulled the ends of his shirt out from his britches. He didn't need to be coddled, but it might be best to see what damage, if any, the colt had done. Most likely his shoulder would be black and blue for a few days.

He grimaced when he had to rotate his shoulder to peel the shirt down his arm. An angry red welt graced the skin.

"An inch over, and you'd have had a busted collarbone," Gus echoed Sam's thoughts. "I'll get some liniment and bandages"

"How about some of Millie's ointment?" Sam grinned when Gus scowled at him.

"Liniment'll work better," he grumbled. He disappeared behind the carriage that had brought Emma Waterston to Three Elms.

36

Sam's jaw clenched. What the hell business did he have thinking about her constantly? No matter where he looked, something reminded him of her. Those tender eyes continued to haunt him.

He removed his cap and raked his fingers through his hair. He had colts to train. He didn't have time to waste on silly thoughts about a woman. Least of all a blueblood like Emmaline Waterston. She was so far out of his league, he might as well make starry eyes at Sally, the goat that kept Dusty company in his stall.

Boots scuffed in the dirt behind him, and Sam shifted his haunches on the straw bale. He frowned. Lonnie Clayton stomped down the barn aisle like an angry vulture.

"Hawley," he roared. "What the hell is Dusty doing out in the paddock when I gave explicit instructions that he wasn't to be turned out?"

Sam slowly rose to his feet. He faced Lonnie squarely and waited for the older man to come to a stop.

"That horse needs to be outside, not confined to a stall," Sam said calmly while anger rose in him.

Lonnie's face reddened and he pointed in the direction from which he'd just come, as if Sam would be able to see Dusty from here.

"That horse is worth more money than you and I combined will ever be worth in ten lifetimes. If he goes lame, we're both out of a job."

"He'll go lame if he's cooped up. He's a big colt, and needs the exercise."

"Then work him harder." Lonnie leaned toward Sam, his hands on his hips.

"I can't work him harder," Sam shot back immediately. "He's still growing, and if you work him too hard, he'll break down. A two-year-old his size needs to be brought along slowly."

37

Sam clenched his jaw. He didn't need to tell the head trainer all of this. Lonnie knew how to train a horse, but he was a spineless coward, always doing David Benton's bidding.

"Look, Sam," Lonnie said in a calmer voice, shifting weight from one foot to the other. "Benton came to me, and wants him to start in his first race in a couple of months. He needs to be ready."

"Tell Benton to shove it." Sam gripped his cap until his knuckles turned white. "He doesn't give a hoot about the horse."

"Well, if you give a hoot about your job, you'd best do what you're told. I, for one, am not going to lose my job because you're trying to coddle that animal. Since you answer to me, do as I tell you."

Sam ground his teeth. He glanced from Lonnie to Gus, who came up behind the head trainer. The old man shook his head in a warning gesture. Sam inhaled a deep breath.

"Let me do my job, Lonnie." His words were as calm as he could muster at the moment. "You know as well as I do that Dusty needs to be brought along slow. He'll be a champion, but not if he breaks down before he's even three years old."

Lonnie's lips tightened. He ran a hand through his hair, then pointed a finger at Sam. "Get that horse ready to race in July, or you're back to mucking stalls."

With those words, he turned and stomped from the barn. Sam tossed his cap on the ground, the swift movement sending a hot jolt of pain through his arm.

"Best not rile him too much." Gus walked up to him, a jar of liniment and a roll of bandages in his hands. "You know he's only doing what David Benton tells him."

"Lonnie's a coward," Sam grumbled and bent to pick up his cap.

He shot one more glance toward the end of the barn where the trainer had disappeared, then returned to the straw bale.

"Yes, he is," Gus confirmed. "But unless you're ready to pick up and move somewhere else, you'd better lie low and do what you're told."

"I'll do what's in the best interest of the horses. I can't train an animal, knowing that I'll be harming him." Sam stared at Gus. The old caretaker knew him better than that.

"And you're going to find a way to do just that, without making the boss angry. It's how I've done it for years." Gus smiled and winked. "Now sit still, so I can take a look at that shoulder."

Chapter Six

Emma glanced at her reflection in the mirror one final time, smoothed her hair in place, and headed out the door of her room and down the stairs. Hopefully she wasn't late for breakfast. No one had knocked to wake her, and from the looks of it outside, it was still early.

She descended the stairs, her skirts swishing around her legs. She wore the last of her good dresses, but it didn't seem good enough for this grand house. Last evening, she'd worn the finer of the two to supper, hoping to make an impression, but David Benton hadn't been there to greet her.

Instead, his mother had told her that it would be just the two of them. David, apparently, had remained in Lexington on business, according to a messenger. Lizette had assured her that he would be home in the morning, and had sent his sincerest apologies.

Emma had forced a smile on her face throughout supper. If David had been in Lexington, why couldn't he have come to the train station to meet her? She'd wanted to ask, but it might have sounded too judgmental.

Men with means acquired their wealth through hard work, and this farm was testament that the owners worked very hard to live the lifestyle they did. Unlike her father, whose laziness and irresponsibility had cost Emma her home. David seemed like a hardworking man, and if he was gone from the estate for a good portion of the time, as Lizzy had said earlier, it would suit Emma just fine.

She'd excused herself shortly after supper, feigning fatigue from travel.

"Of course, dear," Lizzy had smiled at her. "You get a good night's rest, and tomorrow David should be home and the two of you can finally meet." She'd held Emma by the shoulders and kissed her cheek.

40

Emma sighed. Hopefully this morning, she'd meet her fiancé. She turned the corner down the hall, when loud and angry voices drifted through the closed doors of the dining room. Emma hesitated. Lizette was arguing with a man.

"I'm trying to look out for you. How many times do I have to explain that?" Lizette hissed. She certainly didn't sound like the friendly woman Emma had met yesterday. "The reputation of this farm is at stake, and I will not have you ruin your father's good name with your habits."

The man laughed. "I'm not going to be ordered around like one of your servants."

"Emma is a wonderful young woman," Lizette continued, her voice louder this time. "She's just what you need."

Emma stepped up to the door. Her heart pounded in her chest at the sound of her name. Hesitating, she pushed down on the handle. If they were discussing her, she wasn't going to eavesdrop.

Two heads turned when she walked into the large dining room. Lizette stood at the head of the long table, her eyes wide. The man, fitting the description David had sent to her about himself, sat leaning back in a chair. His feet were propped on the table, crossed carelessly at the ankles. The ends of his white shirt hung haphazardly out of his dark trousers, and his hair was a disheveled mess. Even from a distance, his eyes appeared bloodshot.

Emma swallowed her apprehension and stepped fully into the room. The man she assumed was David slowly straightened in his chair and swung his feet down from the table. He stood, but wobbled unsteadily. Lizette rushed around the table toward Emma.

"Emma, dear, how are you this morning?" Lizette held out her hands, but the smile on her face was strained, more so than yesterday. "I hope you had a restful night."

41

"Yes, thank you." Emma accepted the older woman's embrace, but she glanced at the man who stood with his hand on the table, no doubt for support.

Their eyes connected. The man's lips widened in an insolent grin. Lizette ushered her toward the table. "David, I'd like you to finally meet Emma."

Emma's forehead wrinkled and she shot a confused look at David Benton's mother. The introduction seemed backward. He should be introducing her to his mother.

David straightened and pushed away from the table. His eyes raked over her, and Emma swallowed past the throbbing of her heart in her throat. She'd never been looked at the way this man was looking at her, as if he were mentally undressing her. The leer in his eyes grew more intense.

"So, this is my lovely bride-to-be?" He stepped up to her, his hands behind his back. He leaned his body to the left as if appraising her backside.

Emma's spine stiffened. She gritted her teeth. This man was drunk. Lizette's rigid posture next to her, and the way she gripped Emma's arm told her that the older woman was just as apprehensive about this meeting as she.

"Emma, dear, David has had a long night, and is probably exhausted. Perhaps this meeting should be postponed until he's had some rest."

"Why, Mother?" David glared at Lizette. "You were more than eager to shove this lovely lady at me all these weeks. Why postpone our meeting any longer?"

He turned to Emma and took her hand. In a dramatic bow, he kissed the top of her hand, his tongue running up the back of her wrist. Emma gasped and pulled her hand away.

"I must say she's a delectable choice."

Emma stared at him, speechless. A shudder raced down her spine at his insolent, brazen behavior.

"Emma, I'll have Judith get you some breakfast out on the veranda while I speak to my son."

Lizette pushed her toward the glass doors leading outside. Emma stood her ground. She glared from Lizette to David. "I can't say that the pleasure is mine to finally meet you, Mr. Benton, but I'm getting the feeling that not all is as it seems."

David Benton laughed, looking triumphantly at his mother. "Looks like you've got some explaining to do to her, too, Mother. I think I'll just leave you two ladies to it, then, and get some sleep." He leered at Emma again. "It's been a long and exhausting night."

Turning to her, he leaned forward and whispered against her cheek. "You and I will get along just fine. My mother has impeccable taste."

Emma coughed at the stench of bourbon on his breath. She backed away and stared after him when he sauntered out of the room. The instant the door closed behind him, she wheeled to look at Lizette Benton.

"David didn't know about me?"

The truth to Emma's question stared back at her through Lizette's gaze. Anger surged through her.

"Come and sit down, Emma. Have some breakfast, and we'll discuss it." She reached for Emma's hand. Emma yanked it away. She shook her head.

"No, I'd like an explanation. Your son is the rudest, most callous man I have ever had the misfortune to meet. He didn't send for me, did he? Nor write that kind letter to me, asking me to come here."

Her heart sank to her stomach. Panic made bile rise in her throat. She had no money, and nowhere to go.

Lizette looked demure and her lips drew together in an apologetic frown. "I placed the ad in the Gazette on David's behalf," she said slowly. She raised her hand to Emma's arm. "David works hard. He's been a bit wayward

43

lately, I'll admit, but the enormous responsibility of running this estate is the cause for his behavior. I assure you, once he's had some rest, you'll like him. And he will like you."

Emma's forehead scrunched. "Why would you have to place an ad for a wife so far away? Surely there are plenty of women right here in Lexington that would be flattered to be courted by David?"

Lizette blinked. She shook her head slightly. "David doesn't know what he wants. A wife will put him back on the right road. You two will make a wonderful couple."

Emma backed away. Her impulse was to run from the room. She should have followed her intuition, and not answered the ad in the first place. She was worse off now than before. She had no funds to return to the familiarity of Boston.

She inhaled a deep breath to calm her jumbled nerves. She didn't need a perfect husband, only one who would provide financial security. That's why she'd answered that ad.

"You can't leave, Emma." Lizette's face sobered, as if she'd read Emma's thoughts. "I have a seamstress scheduled to arrive today to fit you for a new wardrobe. You will have the finest of everything again."

Emma stared into the eyes of a desperate woman, perhaps more desperate than herself. "What do you mean, 'again'?"

Lizette moved to the dining room table. She lifted her coffee cup, and took a sip. She dabbed at her chin before setting the cup back in its saucer, then straightened.

"Certainly you can understand that we would need to know who we are accepting into our family? We must avoid scandal at any cost. I investigated you before I sent you a reply on David's behalf. I know all about your situation, Emma dear. Your mother is dead, and your father left you with nothing. You can't return to Boston."

Emma expelled a breath of air in disbelief. "You had me investigated?" she whispered. She shivered worse than when David had touched his tongue to her hand.

"You come from a nearly impeccable background, Emma. What happened to you is not your fault, although your father's dealings did leave a small blemish on your family name. However, now you've been given a chance to get back the life you once had. In fact, an even better life."

"I can't believe what I'm hearing." Emma's voice rose in anger. "Why would you deceive me like this?"

Lizette walked up to her again. "I'm offering you a good life, Emma." Her eyes glared and her voice turned cold. "All you have to do is marry my son, be a dutiful wife to him, and make appearances with him in public. In exchange, you will want for nothing."

Emma scoffed. "What if I refuse?"

Lizette gave a triumphant laugh. "You won't refuse, dear. You've lived in poverty too long. I see the hunger in your eyes to get back what you once had. Besides, you have no means to return to Boston."

The woman's placid voice intensified Emma's anger. Lizette calmly lifted her coffee cup, and held it to her lips. She met Emma's stare after setting the cup back on its saucer.

"If you wish to refuse, I will have to ask that you remove yourself from this property immediately."

Emma blinked back the sting of tears in her eyes. Tears of frustration, because this woman knew precisely why she couldn't leave. She inhaled a deep breath. Thoughts raced through her mind so fast, she needed a quiet place to think clearly.

"I've developed a headache," Emma said, resigning herself to her fate. "If you'll excuse me, Lizzy, I think I'll return to my room for a while."

Lizette beamed a genuine smile. "Splendid idea, my dear. I'll have Judith come and get you when my seamstress arrives."

Emma rushed from the room and stumbled up the staircase. She shot a hasty look at the door to David Benton's bedroom, and nearly ran to the seclusion of her own room. She slammed the door too hard, making one of the paintings vibrate on the wall.

"I knew that ad was too good to be true," she mumbled under her breath. No wealthy man would have need to advertise for a wife, unless there was something seriously wrong with him. Hadn't she thought of that many times since reading the ad, and during the long train ride to get to Kentucky?

Emma's heart skipped a beat. David Benton was a drunk. She shuddered at the way he'd leered at her, his bloodshot eyes hungry like those of a predator. Had he simply been out of character because he'd had too much to drink?

She'd encountered drunks before on the streets of Lawrence, on her way home to her apartment from the factory. Usually, she'd walk with at least one or more of the other girls, but that hadn't stopped drunken men from making rude comments to them.

"Gillian, what am I to do?" If only her sensible friend were here right now to offer her some advice.

Willow's voice echoed in her ear, telling her to have faith, and that everything would work out for the best.

"I'm trying to have faith and make the best of it," Emma whispered.

Things could be far worse. She could be out on the streets in Lawrence or Boston. She was being offered a life of luxury, the life she wanted, just as Lizette had said.

Emma gazed out at the pastures. The horses grazing

46

in the fields looked so tranquil, and eased the turmoil in her head. Whenever she'd been upset as a young girl, her horse Ajax had offered her his quiet comfort. Strolling through a barn, inhaling the scent of hay and horses, had always been soothing.

She straightened and a smile passed over her lips. There were barns and dozens of horses right in front of her. Emma dabbed a handkerchief under her eyes and reached for her shawl. Quietly, she opened the door to her room and marched down the hall. Hopefully, Lizette would still be eating her breakfast in the dining room.

Emma glanced up and down the big entry once she was downstairs. She was alone, and didn't have to explain her actions to anyone. She slipped out of the house and followed the gravel road in the direction from which the carriage had come yesterday. With each footfall, the tightness in her chest eased. By the time she approached the first barn, there was a distinct spring to her steps.

She closed her eyes and inhaled the ever-stronger scent of horses. The spring grass gave off a pleasant fragrant smell, and her mood was definitely lifted. A man emerged from the barn, walking with quick strides in the opposite direction. He hadn't even noticed her. Emma glanced around. The horses in the pastures were too far away, but perhaps she could pet one of the stabled animals.

Rounding the corner of the barn, she stepped inside through the wide open doors. The glare of sunlight coming from the open, opposite end of the barn momentarily blinded her. She moved further into the dim barn aisle, around the carriage that had brought her to the Three Elms Farm yesterday.

She blinked to adjust her eyes and her heart nearly came to a stop. Sitting not ten yards away, on a bale of straw, was the man who'd instantly entered her thoughts when she'd seen the carriage.

He sat at an angle while an older man wrapped a bandage around his bare upper chest. Emma's mouth went dry at her glimpse of his broad shoulders, lean upper body, and the corded muscles of his upper arms. She moved to leave, when the older man looked up from his task and smiled warmly.

"Well, looks like we have a visitor," the older man said to Hawley before looking fully at her.

Emma's feet turned to lead. She couldn't move if her life depended on it. Hawley shifted his torso to look in her direction. His head turned slowly and their eyes connected.

Chapter Seven

Emma forced her eyes away from the man whose stare seemed to seep straight into her core. He rose to his feet, a puzzled look on his face. She moved her gaze to the older man, who wore an amused smile. He stepped away from Hawley and toward her. Emma could feel Hawley's eyes on her without even looking at him. Heat crept up her neck and into her cheeks when he slowly stood.

"Is there something we can do for you, Miss?" the older man asked. He walked slightly hunched over and with a noticeable limp.

Emma shook her head. "No," she stammered. "I was just going for a walk. I didn't realize this barn doesn't house horses."

The older man chuckled. He swiped a hand over his balding head. "We keep the Missus' carriages in here, and other equipment. If you're looking for horses, you can find them in the next barn over." He pointed out the other end of the barn from where she'd entered.

"Thank you." Emma plastered a smile on her face. "I'll be going, then. Thank you for pointing me in the right direction."

"Anytime, Miss. Everyone here calls me Gus, and if you need anything that has to do with the horses, you come see me."

"All right." Emma nodded at the kind old man. "I won't keep you from your work."

Gus chuckled. "No trouble at all, Miss. After all, you'll be the new missus around here soon enough, am I right?"

Emma looked into the man's wrinkled face. His eyes sparkled and his brows rose. After meeting her future husband a short while ago, the title of missus of this estate sounded less appealing than it had yesterday.

"Emmaline Waterston," she said without committing to an answer to his question.

"Emma. Now that's a right pretty name, don't you think so, Sam?" Gus turned his head to look at the man who stood silently in front of the straw bale.

Emma's eyes moved to him before she could even stop her actions. Her heart thumped against her ribs. Hawley was still staring at her. Rather than shivers of apprehension like what she'd experienced from David's rude stares, Hawley's gaze sent a decidedly different thrill down her spine.

Twice in one day now, men had looked at her with an appraising eye. While David's stare had done nothing but make her feel exposed, the admiring glance from Hawley left her feeling warm all over.

She forced her eyes back on Gus. His familiar use of her name left her without a reply momentarily. The servants in Boston wouldn't dare speak so casually to their employers. Strangely, it didn't bother her. Gus was immediately likable, and Emma returned his warm smile.

"It's what my friends back home always called me," she almost whispered.

A sharp twinge of homesickness engulfed her. She'd come here with high hopes of finding a new life, establishing new roots and securing a future. All she'd found so far was a man who'd made less than a favorable impression on her, and his manipulative mother.

"I'm sure you're missing them right about now," Gus said. He couldn't have known how true his statement was at that moment. Emma blinked back that familiar sting in the back of her eyes. She wasn't a weepy woman, but today, vulnerability and loneliness won out over keeping her chin up and her emotions hidden.

"I should probably go, and leave you to your work," she said hastily, before she made a fool of herself in front of this man and the one still watching her in silence. "It was a pleasure meeting you, Gus."

She was about to leave the barn when a loud voice behind her made her turn.

"There you are," a large woman bellowed, and came sauntering into the barn.

Emma frowned, then looked to Gus, whose eyes had gone wide with an appreciative gleam.

"I thought you'd be at your cottage, resting that rheumatism of yours. My salve must have worked yesterday."

Gus smiled sheepishly. "It worked wonders, Millie," he confirmed, and rubbed at the back of his neck.

She held out a basket to Gus. "I brought a freshly baked loaf of bread. I made extra, but no one seemed to want my cooking this morning."

The woman, Millie, swept her gaze toward Emma and her eyes widened.

"Well, land sakes," she said with her hand on her wide hip. "You'd rather be traipsing around the barn than eat my good food, Miss Emma?"

Emma blinked and looked around to confirm the woman was addressing her. She'd never seen this woman before, but she was obviously part of the kitchen staff. She shook her head to clear her mind.

"I beg your pardon?"

"Miz Lizzy told me you'd lost your appetite this morning, and sent breakfast back to the kitchen." The woman advanced on her with both hands on her hips. "No one sends my food back."

Emma's spine stiffened. She opened her mouth to tell this woman to mind her place, when Millie's face transformed from looking murderous to flashing a wide smile. Her matronly eyes swept over Emma and she pulled her against her heaving bosom in a tight embrace.

"I knew you the minute I set eyes on you," she said in a loud tone. "Miz Lizzy told me last night what a pretty thing you are, and she wasn't telling stories at all."

She straightened and held Emma at arm's length, appraising her with warm eyes. Emma coughed and inhaled a quick breath in case the woman planned to suffocate her again. No one had ever hugged her like this before, least of all a servant. Rather than finding it off-putting, something squeezed in Emma's heart and she returned the woman's smile.

"No wonder you're such a little thing if you don't eat," Millie continued. "When you get back up to the house you stop in the kitchen, and I'm gonna fix you right up with a good plate of food." She nodded at her own words, then turned her eyes on Gus when he chuckled.

"Millie's cooking will put some meat on your bones right quick," the old man confirmed.

Millie glared at his waist. "And by the looks of you, you ain't complaining, old man."

Gus shook his head and rubbed at his belly. "Never complained about your cooking."

A spark of affection flashed in Millie's eyes, and Emma darted glances from her to Gus. Millie turned her attention to the man Emma had nearly forgotten about.

"And what do you think you're doing, standing around half naked in front of a lady, Sam Hawley?"

Hawley shifted his weight and an easy grin formed on his lips, causing indents in his cheeks. Emma's heart fluttered. He was by far the most handsome man she'd ever seen. She blinked away her silly thoughts and returned her attention to the buxom woman and old man.

Emma smiled inwardly. These were common people, much like the ones she'd associated with since working in

52

the factory. Although she hadn't considered most of them close friends, she admired their camaraderie and their casual banter. The way they interacted was so different from what she'd grown up knowing.

"I was doctoring up his shoulder," Gus grumbled.

Millie squeezed her lips together and frowned. She walked up to Sam and unwrapped the bandage from around his chest and shoulder, appraising it with a critical eye.

Emma's eyes widened when Sam's entire chest was exposed to her view. Her pulse quickened. She'd only seen one nude male chest before. Some drunk on the streets of Lawrence had provided a sight she'd much rather forget. Taking in this man's physique, even with the angry red mark on his shoulder, a new appreciation formed for the nude sculptures she'd seen in museums.

When Sam looked at her, she quickly dropped her gaze, but not before she caught the widening of his smile.

"You let that old coot near you with a hurt shoulder?" Millie droned. She leaned forward, her nose nearly touching Sam's skin, and made a face when she smelled him. She quickly straightened and waved her hand in front of her.

"What's he doing? Rubbing horse liniment on you?" She glared from Sam to Gus. "You want to lose the use of your arm for good, boy?"

Emma's eyes widened when the woman reached out with her hand to cuff the side of Sam's head. He must have seen her intent, for he ducked quickly and avoided the swat.

"I want you to come up to the kitchen, and I'll put something on that shoulder that will actually help it heal."

"Yes, ma'am," Sam said, still grinning. By the sound of his tone, he had no intention of doing what Millie ordered. And by the disapproving frown on her face, she

53

didn't believe he would, either.

"Well." The wide woman glanced at Gus. "I have to get back to the house. Supper won't cook itself, and I have preparations to make." Her gaze moved to Emma.

"I hope you like burgoo, 'cause it's my specialty."

Emma shook her head. "My apologies. I've never heard of it."

Gus smacked his lips, and Millie scoffed. "Well, it don't matter. You'll love mine. And I add in a healthy dose of bourbon, so it'll settle right in your belly." She sauntered toward the wide, open barn doors. "Bring that basket back to the house when you're done eating my bread, Gus Ferguson."

"I always do," he called after her and peered into the basket, lifting the cloth that covered the contents.

"Would you care for some of Millie's fresh bread, Miss Emma?" Gus held the basket up to her.

Emma shook her head. Now that Millie was gone, tension returned to her insides, and Sam's eyes on her weighed her to the ground.

"I'd best be going, too. It was nice meeting you, Gus." Emma hesitated for a second, then held out her hand to the old man. He shook it, his weathered fingers closing over hers like a warm glove.

"The pleasure is all mine, Miss, and I'm sure we'll see you around again."

Emma nodded and offered a weak smile. She shot a hasty glance at Hawley. Her cheeks flamed the instant she took notice of him.

It was time to leave this barn, but returning to the house made her stomach turn.

"Hawley." She nodded curtly, without looking at him, and left through the barn doors at the other end, which led to the rest of the stables.

54

* * *

"Heard anything from your cousin lately?" Gus asked, and finished wrapping the bandage around Sam's chest that Millie had removed.

Sam glanced over his shoulder. "Trace?"

Gus nodded.

It was a silly question. He didn't have any other cousins. Trace Hawley was his deceased Uncle Paul's son, and owner of one of the wealthiest thoroughbred ranches in Montana. Sam shook his head. He'd only met his cousin a couple of times.

The last time had been two years ago, when he'd brought a colt from Montana to the Derby and had made fools out of all the Kentucky bluebloods. Everyone had scoffed and laughed at him, and told him to take his 'cow horse' back to cattle country. One look at the colt, and Sam had known that the Derby would go to Montana that year.

He smiled at the memory. Mrs. Benton's heavy favorite had failed to run that day, and David Benton had sold the horse at the first opportunity. Trace had shown them all that it wasn't always about who had the most money, even though Trace had plenty of money.

"Sure is something, what he's done with his life and what he's accomplished." Gus shook his head and smiled. "Married that pretty heiress, and got himself a prosperous horse ranch along with the girl."

Sam's eyes narrowed. Where was the old coot going with that?

"I don't think Trace cared about the money. He loves Katie. That was obvious when we saw them a couple of years ago." Sam tried to set him straight. Surely Gus wasn't implying that Trace had married his wife for financial reasons?

Gus chuckled. "Ain't that the truth? I remember him

55

doting on his wife. Incredible to think that she's blind, and gets around as well as she does. The right woman sure has a way of taking hold of a man's heart."

It was Sam's turn to chuckle. "Exactly, Gus. Maybe you should tell Millie that, and get to marrying her."

Gus's eyes widened. "I wasn't talking about Millie, boy." He cleared his throat and stepped away from Sam. He glanced down the barn aisle to where Miss Waterston had disappeared. "Maybe you oughta show that pretty lady around the barns, rather than letting her get lost."

Gus sank his teeth into a thick slice of bread. He closed his eyes and groaned with pleasure when he chewed.

Sam rotated his shoulder, suppressing a hiss at the throbbing ache. The liniment was working to ease the pain, but the shoulder would be stiff for several days. He touched the bandage Gus had re-applied after Millie and . . . Emma had left. Slipping an arm through his shirt, he stood.

"I don't think I'm the right person to give the lady a tour of the farm, Gus." Sam buttoned his shirt and tucked the ends into his britches.

He glanced out the doors toward the broodmare barn. It was the first barn Miss Waterston would find. His feet itched to follow her. That she'd come to the stables had surprised the hell out of him, and the shocked look on her face when she'd seen him still made him smile. The rosy blush to her cheeks didn't go unnoticed.

"And why not? She seems like a nice lady, not as uppity as Miz Benton." Gus paused and shook his head. "Why, it's almost a shame that she –"

The old man cut off his own words, but there was no doubt that he'd wanted to say that it was a shame that she was spoken for by David Benton. Sam mentally shook his head. He'd asked himself a thousand times, but he was asking again. What was a lady like her doing marrying a bastard like Benton? He'd mistreat her like he mistreated everything else. Sam clenched his jaw at the thought.

She clearly liked horses, if she'd come all the way to the barns on her own. He'd seen it when she'd petted the carriage horses, and the soft way she'd spoken to them. That knowledge immediately set her apart from all the other bluebloods with whom he'd associated over the years. Most of them didn't think of the horses as anything but a commodity that made them money. Benton was one of the worst.

Sam reached for a slice of bread and adjusted his cap on his head. No doubt he was about to make a big mistake.

"I'll go and make sure she stays out of trouble, and that the hands behave themselves," he mumbled and headed down the barn aisle, as Gus chuckled softly behind him.

Chapter Eight

Emma walked down the spacious barn aisle, inhaling the pungent odor of hay and horses. A smile passed over her lips, and that familiar tranquil feeling flowed through her. How she'd missed this smell. It seemed even stronger among the other fragrances of Kentucky. The sweet smell of bluegrass simply permeated the air around her. How different this was from living in the city, and working from sunup to sundown in a textile factory.

She'd still be in Lawrence if not for that fire, and so would her friends. Although the factory burning down had been a tragedy, and had put so many women out of work, it had been a blessing in disguise for Willow and Gillian. They were both happily married as a result of it. Rose would have arrived in Colorado by now, and met her new husband. Willow had blamed herself for the fire initially, thinking she'd been careless with a lamp, but the truth about what had really happened soon became apparent.

Emma scoffed. Another man's greed had uprooted so many women. Just like her father's greed and gambling away her mother's wealth had uprooted her.

"You've risen above it all, Emma. You can do it again," she whispered. Even if it meant marrying David Benton. Perhaps once he'd slept off the alcohol, he'd be more likable. She'd come here for one reason, and that was to escape her current life of poverty. Her mother and father hadn't had a close marriage, far from it. They'd hardly ever spent time in each other's company. It would be the same for her, which was perfectly fine.

She glanced around. Emma stood in the empty barn aisle, and an unexpected wave of loneliness swept through her. She'd been here not even a full day, and the most comfortable she'd felt since her arrival had been in that carriage barn, with Millie the cook, and Gus the caretaker.

Most likely it was simply the transition back to her former life. After a year of living in a cramped apartment, she wasn't used to being among the wealthy again.

Working-class people, those with whom she'd been forced to mingle for a year, were genuine and caring, something that hadn't occurred to her until this morning. Even though they didn't have much in the form of money or material goods, they were happy.

Just like you were happy with Rose, Willow, and Gillian.

They'd all worked long hours, and had needed to watch every penny, but they'd had fun, and a great friendship. Things she'd never had with any of her friends in Boston. Every single one of the ladies she'd considered her friends had cut ties with her when they'd found out that she'd lost everything.

Emma laughed softly. For a year, she'd cursed her life every single day and had longed for her home in Boston, her servants, and her old so-called friends. Now she had most of that back, and something about it didn't feel right.

Her vision blurred. Emma glanced around and blinked away her tears of frustration. She should be happy, not weepy. What on earth had gotten into her? David Benton's leering stare flashed in her mind and her wrist burned with the sensation of his tongue on her skin.

She brushed the feeling aside. She was done being poor. She'd simply have to endure some unpleasantries in exchange for living a life of comfort. Lizette Benton had said that David was gone on business for much of the time. That would suit her just fine.

A chestnut horse with a wide blaze stuck its head over the stall door and nickered softly. Emma sniffed. She squared her shoulders, smiled and headed for the horse.

"Aren't you a pretty one," she said, and reached her hand out to touch the horse's muzzle.

Emma stepped closer and peered into the stall. "And by the looks of your round belly, you're going to have a foal soon."

"She's due to drop her foal any day."

Emma spun around. Her heart jumped up into her throat at the deep, familiar voice behind her. Hawley walked into the barn, and Emma swallowed. Relief swept through her that he'd put his shirt on again, but her cheeks heated at the memory of seeing him standing in the carriage barn with his torso exposed.

What was it about this man that made her feel all nervous and jumbled up inside? Just because he was handsome shouldn't make her all knotted-up. There'd been plenty of handsome men who'd called on her, when she'd still had money, and none of them had affected her this way. Hawley was a servant, a mere stable hand. She shouldn't be in this barn, alone with him, and he should know better, too.

Rather than leaving, Hawley moved closer, but his steps slowed. Emma glanced around. Too bad Millie or someone else didn't come to her rescue, but the barn was deserted, other than the horses. He reached into his shirt pocket and held his hand out to the mare. She stretched her neck and accepted the treat he offered, chewing eagerly.

"Even the horses love Millie's bread," he said with a smile. He patted the mare's neck as she stretched, searching for more treats.

Emma blinked and shook her head slightly to keep from staring at him. This was highly improper. Why had he followed her? She moved to leave, then stopped. Why should she leave? She wasn't ready to return to the house and listen to Lizette drone on about engagement parties and dresses. Before she realized it, a soft laugh escaped her lips at the irony of it.

For a year she'd cursed her father for forcing her out of her lifestyle. Now, here she was, and what she thought she'd been missing was being handed to her, yet she was standing in a stable, alone, talking to a stable hand. And suddenly, she didn't care about the impropriety.

Back in Boston, the hired help wouldn't have dared come up to her and start a conversation without being addressed first. Perhaps here in Kentucky, the social norms weren't quite as strict.

"Something funny?" Hawley's brows rose, making his forehead wrinkle. He removed his cap and ran his fingers through his disheveled mop of hair.

"No," she said quickly. "I just haven't been around horses in a long time, and I've really missed it." Her smile faded.

"Well, there's plenty of horses here for you to see whenever you want."

Hawley directed his attention to the horse, running his hand along the mare's neck.

Emma forced her eyes away from the man's hand stroking the animal. She lifted her own hand to touch the soft muzzle. The mare blew warm air onto her wrist.

"What's her name?" she asked, avoiding eye contact with Hawley. There was a slight pause before he answered.

"Her name is One Lucky Lady, but we just call her the Queen."

Emma patted the mare's forehead. "I think she knows she's a queen."

Beside her, Sam chuckled. "She does get the royal treatment. We're keeping a close eye on her. Her foal last year was stillborn."

Emma briefly glanced up at Hawley. "That's terrible. Nothing's going to happen this time, is it?"

He shrugged. "Hard to tell. I just wish Benton-" He

61

broke off in mid-sentence and his face hardened.

"You wish David Benton, what?" Emma prodded.

Sam adjusted his cap on his head before answering. "He shouldn't have ordered her bred again so soon." His voice took on a note of anger. "She's produced eight foals already, one each year. Her body needs a rest."

Emma raised her eyes to his. Hawley was a good head taller than she, and he stood much too close. He spoke with such passion, it was evident that he truly cared for the mare.

The odor of liniment and the scent of hay filled her nose. She took a step to the side and dropped her hand from touching the mare.

"Your shoulder," she said, clearing her throat. "I hope it's nothing serious."

Hawley's eyes held hers for longer than was proper in any social circles, and Emma swallowed past the growing lump in her throat. She shouldn't have asked. She shouldn't be lingering in the barn. Finally, he shifted his shoulder and smiled, which was partly a grimace.

"Rambunctious colt got me." He chuckled. "In fact, it was this mare's two-year old. All part of the job of training young horses. They can be unruly, and unpredictable."

Emma's eyes widened. "You're a trainer, Hawley?"

His grin turned genuine, and butterflies churned in her belly. A horse trainer certainly held a higher ranking than a mere stable hand.

"Sometimes I drive the carriage when Gus asks me." There was definite humor in his voice and a twinkle in his eye. Clearly, he was referring to being her driver yesterday. "Everyone calls me Sam, by the way."

Emma shook her head. "I don't think it's appropriate to be on a first name basis." She glanced around and moved away from the stall. "Or that you and I are in this barn together, alone."

A hint of annoyance passed over him. "I don't bite, Miss Waterston. I came in here to be polite to a newcomer to the farm." He scoffed and shook his head. "And here I thought for a second that you were different from them."

Emma's brows drew together. "Different?"

"Yeah. None of those rich folks at the house give a hoot about the horses. I saw you pet those carriage horses yesterday, and now you're here in the barn. Lizette Benton comes to the stables once a year, when she's showing off her prized horses she knows nothing about to investors with deep pockets."

Emma took another step back to put some distance between herself and Sam Hawley. He hadn't even bothered to disguise the contempt in his voice.

"I do care about horses," she stammered for lack of something else to say. She raised her chin and her spine stiffened. "I had a horse growing up."

Emma challenged him with her stare. She didn't owe this man an explanation. "I think you're out of line, Hawley," she added with as much force as she could muster, emphasizing his last name.

He shook his head as if something had just occurred to him, and laughed scornfully. "My apologies, Miss Waterston," he said, sounding anything but apologetic. The muscles along his jaw tightened. "Since it's improper to talk to you, please excuse me. I've got work to do."

He tipped the brim of his cap with his index and middle fingers, nodded curtly, and marched from the barn. Emma stared after him. Relief should have been her first reaction that he was leaving, but it was regret that flowed through her. Regret for trying to put him in his proper place. Emma mentally shook her head. He was nothing but a rude barn employee, even if she'd pegged him wrong about his job title.

63

She faced the horse, turning away from the man's retreating form, but his words lingered in her mind. He'd thought she was different from the Bentons.

Emma scoffed. How right he was. She was different from them. At least she hadn't forgotten how to act like a convincing member of the elite. She'd obviously fooled Hawley . . . Sam.

Patting the mare's nose a final time, she sighed, and slipped out of the barn, leaving through the opposite doors that Hawley had taken. At least no one had seen her in the barn, alone with the hired help. No doubt Lizzy Benton was looking for her at this point.

Inhaling deeply, she made her way back to the house, and an afternoon filled with dress fittings and sipping tea with her future mother-in-law. Perhaps she could slip away for a while and write a letter to her friends.

Chapter Nine

Sam rotated his shoulder and hissed. He worked his arm into the sleeve of his shirt and stood from sitting on his bunk. It had been three days since Dusty had struck him with his hoof, and the pain hadn't gone away. Gus had rubbed liniment on it every day and kept it wrapped, but it hadn't helped.

At least the colt had settled down. Lonnie had seen that Sam had turned Dusty out for several hours each day, but hadn't approached him again. David Benton had left on some so-called business a few days ago. To the best of Sam's knowledge, he hadn't been back. With Benton gone, Lonnie had been a lot more agreeable to Sam's training methods.

Sam shook his head, his mind drifting to other things again besides Dusty's training. Why had Benton left the farm when his fiancée had just arrived? The bastard had no appreciation for anything or anyone. Apparently, he had the same attitude toward his future wife. He shrugged. Why did he waste time even thinking about . . . her?

Sam left his room and glanced around the small kitchen of the cottage he shared with Gus. The old man poured two mugs of steaming coffee, then faced Sam and held one out to him. Sam reached for it with his left hand out of habit. He grimaced at the pain the action brought to his arm.

"Maybe you oughta go see Millie. Don't look like the liniment is helping."

"I'll be fine in another few days." Sam sipped at the bitter brew.

Gus tilted his head and shot him a quizzical stare. "It ain't like you to be so stubborn," he remarked. With a groan, he lowered himself into one of the kitchen chairs. "You're always chastising me for not taking care of my aches and pains. Maybe you oughta take your own advice."

Sam walked to the window and stared out. From where he stood, the path leading up to the big house was visible through the foliage of the trees. The early morning sun reflected off the mist that hovered over the pastures, giving the grass an almost blue hue like its name implied. He sipped at his coffee again.

"Might there be a different reason why you're so dead set against going up to the main house?" The snigger in Gus' question was easy to hear. Sam didn't have to turn to see that the old man had a grin on his face.

"I never go up to the main house. You know that," Sam grumbled.

"You also never had a busted-up shoulder before and needed Millie's care," Gus prodded. "Might you be afraid of running into one young lady who's taken up residence there?"

Sam turned to face his mentor. The old man's eyes twinkled with amusement.

"Don't be a fool," Sam said, more forcefully than he'd intended. Of course that was the reason he didn't want to go and see Millie for some relief to his aching shoulder. Why did Gus have to point it out?

"She seems like a nice lady." Gus shrugged. "Might be just what this farm needs."

Sam coughed to suppress the string of swear words that came to mind. He'd thought the same thing about her, but her true colors had emerged when he'd tried to talk to her three days ago in the broodmare barn. He'd wanted to believe she was different, because for some reason he couldn't explain, he'd been instantly attracted to her, as ludicrous as the notion was. His kind didn't mingle with her kind, and she'd set him straight about that real quick when she'd told him he was out of line.

"She's a blueblood, like the rest of them," Sam scoffed. "Why would I want to associate with the likes of her?"

"Why, indeed?" The old man's bushy brows rose. He shook his head and chuckled. "The sparks were purely flying between the two of you the other day in the barn, the way you were looking at each other. I thought the straw you were sitting on might catch fire."

"You're seeing things, old man," Sam grumbled. "And if not for everything I've mentioned, there's also that little detail that she's engaged to someone."

Someone you loathe.

Sam's muscles tensed even more, making his shoulder throb.

Gus laughed heartily. "There's some things that can't be explained, or ignored." He stood and his face turned serious. He touched his hand to Sam's good shoulder. "I wish things were different. David Benton doesn't deserve a lady like Miss Emma."

Sam cracked a smile for the first time to disguise the conflicting emotions whirling through his mind. "You're right. Benton doesn't deserve her, but she's marrying him. And even if she wasn't, she comes from different stock than you or I. Thoroughbreds and mules don't mix, Gus."

Gus nodded, apparently agreeing with him. This discussion was leading nowhere. The old man raised his eyes to look directly at him.

"Your cousin, Trace, married a thoroughbred, and I believe he's a mule just like you." He winked.

Sam frowned and swallowed the last of his coffee. He moved to the door. Time to get to work. He pulled his coat from the peg hanging on the wall and slipped his left arm into the sleeve. A sharp hiss escaped his mouth when pain seared through his shoulder at the movement.

"Go and see Millie," Gus ordered from behind him.

"The training can wait. You need to get that shoulder doctored proper, or you'll be useless handling crazy two-year-old colts."

Sam clenched his jaw. Gus was right. There was no reason he couldn't visit the kitchen at the big house for a few minutes and see if Millie had a special salve that could ease the pain in his shoulder. He'd be no use handling young horses in his condition. He'd slip in through the servants' entrance, which led right into the kitchen. Why hadn't he thought of that before?

"Fine, I'll go see Millie," he relented, and tossed a smile over his shoulder before closing the door behind him. "I'll send her your love, and tell her you need some more of her healing hands yourself."

Sam headed up the path that led to the house. His eyes had been on Miss Waterston walking along this path three days ago when she'd left the mare barn. He gritted his teeth and cursed under his breath. Why had he even followed her into the broodmare barn that day?

He'd known it was a mistake to do what Gus had suggested, and talk to her. Truth was, though, he'd never wanted to talk to a woman more than he'd wanted to talk to this one. There was something about her that had drawn him to Emmaline . . . Emma, from the first moment he'd glimpsed her at the train station in Lexington. Even if she acted all uppity like a Kentucky blueblood, there was something different about her that he hadn't been able to put a finger on, yet.

Best to get your mind back on the horses and away from a woman you have no business giving a second glance.

He chuckled. He'd done plenty of glancing and staring at her already. And it had to stop. She was as unattainable to him as owning a horse like Dusty someday.

The backdoor to the kitchen of the estate stood slightly ajar when he approached, allowing Millie's loud voice to clearly drift outside.

"Pecan Pie is best made with bourbon," Millie boomed. "And I add enough that you'll definitely taste it." She laughed. "No one complains about my Pecan Pie."

"Have you ever made Boston Cream Pie?"

Sam stopped in his tracks. That soft voice belonged to the very person he'd wanted to avoid. What was she doing in the kitchens?

"Never heard of it," Millie said. "But if we can add some good ole Kentucky bourbon to the recipe, I'll gladly try it."

"It's more of a cake, actually, than a pie, but I think I remember how to make it," Emma said, her voice rising with enthusiasm. She laughed softly. "I tried to make it once, for my cousin Rose's birthday, but I'm afraid neither I nor my friends were very adept at cooking. Gillian was the only competent one, but she wasn't available to help at the time. I'm not sure what it was that I ended up serving Rose."

Millie chuckled heartily. "Girl, if you tell me what goes in it, I can make it."

"That would be wonderful. It was always my favorite dessert growing up."

Emma's voice beamed with happiness. Sam stood rooted to the spot. He shouldn't be here, eavesdropping.

"I'll tell you the ingredients, at least what I remember, if you let me help and show me the proper way to bake a cake."

Millie laughed again. "You sure have been a ray of sunshine around this house, Miss Emma. Miz Benton is a decent lady, but she don't cotton to cooking. She likes her fancy things, and has good taste in food, but she don't come to the kitchen."

69

"I've learned how to cook a little, out of necessity." Emma said almost hesitantly as if she didn't want to reveal too much.

"Well, I'll be glad to teach you some of my tricks. As long as I won't be out of a job once you become the mistress of the house."

There was a long pause, then Millie spoke again. "It's gonna be all right," she said, her words softer than she'd ever spoken.

"I don't know, Millie. I'm afraid I've made a big mistake, coming here."

"I don't understand David Benton," Millie chided. "He's got a pretty soon-to-be-wife he ought to be spending time with, yet he rides away for days. Miz Benton thought getting her boy a wife would keep him home more."

Sam clenched his jaw. If he had any sense at all, he'd head back down the road toward the barns. He had no business listening in on this conversation, but he couldn't leave, hearing Emma's soft voice.

"It'll all work out," Millie said quietly.

There was no doubt she was holding back and wanted to say more. Millie had never said a kind word about David Benton. Her sentiments about the man were the same as Sam's.

"Thank you for offering to teach me how to cook."

Sam had to strain his ears to really hear her softly spoken words. "Lizette's got me standing for measurements for hours at a time, and it's making my back sore." She laughed. "I never thought I'd get tired of wardrobe fittings."

"Glad to help," Millie chortled. "It's nice to have company in the kitchen once in a while. The maids don't like to come in here, 'cause they tell me I'm too bossy." Millie chuckled heartily. "I'm sure there's other ways for you to spend your time other than being poked and

70

prodded with needles, or sneaking in here."

There was a short pause before Emma replied. "I would love to visit the horses some more. I used to go riding in Boston and I really miss it. Lizette doesn't seem to care for riding. I suggested it to her, but she told me she doesn't ride."

Millie chuckled again. "Miz Benton is afraid of horses."

Her voice drew closer. Too late for Sam to react, the door opened wider, and Millie stepped out with a pan in her hand. She swung her arms back and tossed the contents onto the ground. Sam jumped back just in time to avoid the spray of dirty dish water.

"Whoa." Sam held out his hands in front of him as if fending off an attack. The quick action caused pain to rip through his shoulder.

Millie's eyes widened and she glared at him. "Sam Hawley, what on earth are you doing, standing outside this door?"

Sam lifted the cap from his head and ran his hand through his hair. He'd been caught like a peeping tom.

"I was coming to see you," he grumbled quickly. It wasn't his fault that the door had been partly open to where he could hear the conversation. Millie didn't have to know how long he'd been standing there, listening.

Millie's hand shot to her hip and she narrowed her eyes on him. "Since when do you come and see me here at the big house? You avoid this place like the plague." She paused, then a wave of concern washed over her face. She grabbed his arm. "It's not Gus, is it? Is he all right?"

Sam grinned. "Gus is fine, but he wanted me to come and tell you that his horse liniment isn't working on my shoulder. And, that he misses your food."

A smug smile passed over Millie's lips and she tilted her head. "So, you finally come and see me, huh? Been three days since that colt got you, isn't it? You must be in some serious pain, boy."

She stepped aside to make room for him to enter the kitchen and waved her hand to speed him along. Sam's heart pounded inexplicably. He entered the spacious kitchen and his gaze instantly fell to the woman sitting on a stool along Millie's long workbench.

Emma watched him walk in, a curious look in her eyes. Her back straightened and she held his gaze.

"Miss Waterston," Sam said stiffly, for lack of another greeting.

"Hawley." She nodded.

"Sam," he corrected before she finished saying his last name.

Her eyes didn't waver from his challenging stare. Sam's lips twitched. She sure was a spunky thing. His heart sped up like a young colt racing for the homestretch.

Millie shot curious glances from him to Emma. Her hands were on her hips and her lips pressed together in a knowing smirk.

"Pull up a chair and sit down, Sam. You're gonna have to take off that shirt so I can look at your shoulder."

Emma shot from her seat as if she'd sat in a pile of fire ants.

"I'd best get going. I'm sure Lizette is looking for me by now. The seamstress is supposed to be here today with more dress alterations."

Millie nodded. "We'll work on your Boston Cream Pie tomorrow. If this boy comes to see me for an injured shoulder, I know he's hurting, and I'd best take care of it."

Emma smiled softly. There was a distinct note of sadness in her eyes. They didn't sparkle the way they had the day she was in the barn.

"I'm looking forward to it. I'll write down a list of ingredients. I just hope I can remember them all."

Millie waved her off. "As long as I know the basic ingredients, I can make anything taste good, ain't that right, Sam?"

He nodded dutifully. Emma's smile brightened. "I know you'll take Boston Cream Pie to new heights." Her eyes moved to Sam and she nodded before turning to leave.

"Sam," she said.

Sam raised his eyebrows that she'd called him by his given name. He caught himself in time before calling her Emma in return.

"Miss Waterston."

"Say, Miss Emma." Millie's voice was slow, almost calculating.

Emma turned to look at the cook, her brows raised.

"You were asking about going riding," Millie continued. Her eyes moved discretely to Sam for a fraction of a second and that smugness passed over her lips again. "You ought to ask Gus next time you visit the barn to recommend someone to take you for a ride. Seeing as you told me you'd like to get out of the house and go horseback riding."

Emma's eyes widened. Her gaze drifted to Sam before quickly making eye contact with Millie again. "I will," she stammered, and hurried from the kitchen.

Millie chuckled, obviously satisfied about something.

"Sit down, boy, and get your head out of the clouds." She pushed him toward the chair Emma had occupied a minute ago.

Sam stared at the door through which Emma disappeared. He unbuttoned his shirt while Millie rummaged through her cupboards.

"I think I've made a big mistake."

Emma's words from earlier came back to him. Was she having second thoughts about marrying Benton?

Nothing would make him happier, knowing she wouldn't be with Benton, but that didn't mean anything where he was concerned. A blueblood didn't mingle with the hired help. There was that little matter of coming from different social classes for him to associate with her.

Sam shook his head and peeled his shirt off, then braced himself for Millie's ministrations to his injured shoulder.

Chapter Ten

Emma folded the last sheet of paper and stuffed it in its proper envelope, which was already addressed to Rose. Gillian's and Willow's letters were sealed. All she had to do now was ask Lizzy if someone could deliver the letters to Lexington so they could get mailed.

She rose from her seat and moved to the door leading to the balcony. Looking out at the fields each morning had become a ritual, and today she wasn't going to sit in this great big house with nothing to do. She'd pestered Millie enough in the kitchen over the last few days.

To her great astonishment, the talented cook had produced a Boston Cream Pie that rivaled anything she'd tasted at home. Although, true to her word, Millie had added a generous dose of bourbon which had added to the cake's rich flavor.

Emma buttoned up her shirtwaist and reached for the new pair of leather gloves on her dresser. The riding skirt she wore had arrived just yesterday. Lizette's seamstress truly did remarkable work, in a short amount of time. She glanced at her reflection in the mirror and smiled despite the constant feeling of dread that she'd made a terrible mistake in answering the ad to become David Benton's wife.

He'd been gone for nearly a week. No one seemed to be concerned about his absence, especially the house staff. Millie had cut off mid-sentence several times when their conversations had turned to David. There were things she clearly didn't want to say about her employer. No doubt, if he behaved as badly all the time as he had during their one and only brief meeting, Emma could well understand. On the up side, his extended absences from the estate meant she didn't have to spend any time with him.

Emma pinned her hat to her head and left the room. Lizette was eating breakfast in the dining room when Emma entered. The older woman's eyes swept over her with a satisfied smile.

"You look lovely, my dear," she beamed, and indicated for her to sit. "Have some breakfast with me. Millie is rather put out that you don't seem to enjoy her cooking."

Emma smiled and shook her head to decline the offer.

"Millie knows I like her cooking. She also knows I prefer not to eat in the morning. I think she's slowly coming around to that idea."

Lizette nodded. "Your outfit looks nice. Hetty has done a wonderful job on your wardrobe so far." She sipped her coffee and her eyes sparkled with excitement. "The material for your wedding gown should arrive any day."

A quick jolt of apprehension at the word wedding seeped through Emma, but she plastered a smile on her face.

"Are you sure you don't mind that I go to the stables this morning?"

Even if Lizette answered in the negative, Emma would find a way to get to the barns. The temptation of the horses beckoning to her from her view on the balcony had grown stronger every day.

"Of course not, dear," Lizette sang. "I can have Judith escort you to the carriage house, where you'll find Gus. He's been the caretaker and my family's personal driver here at the Three Elms for nearly forty years. I trust him explicitly. Without him, I'm afraid half of my staff and stable help would walk out on me." Lizette chuckled.

She stood and strode over to Emma, patting her arm.

"David will be back any day now. I'm sure he'd be delighted to take you for a ride and show you the grounds, but I see that you're restless. Gus will find a trustworthy groom to escort you."

"Did someone say my name?"

Emma's head snapped around to the entry, where David Benton strode into the room with long, sweeping strides. Her eyes widened. He looked noticeably different than the last time she'd seen him. Dressed impeccably in a dark blue suit, he wore a bright smile. His gaze swept from his mother and settled on Emma. She swallowed.

"Hello, Mother," he said, and bowed slightly before Lizette. He kissed the top of her hand, then turned his attention on Emma.

His eyes roamed over her appreciatively. Although there was no hint that he was drunk, there was something dark in his stare, like some hungry predator on the prowl. He took her hand in his and held it to his lips. His gaze held hers while his mouth lingered on the top of her hand.

"I almost forgot how absolutely lovely you are, Emma. I do apologize for my behavior the other day. I hope we can start fresh, and pretend that incident never happened."

Emma caught the wide-eyed look on Lizette's face before she turned her full attention to her intended husband.

"I would like that." She offered an uneasy smile.

Her heart drummed against her ribs, not in an exhilarated way, but one laced with trepidation, and she tugged her hand back from his grip. His overly-friendly demeanor was unsettling. The memory of another man's face obscured her vision of David.

Sam Hawley had an unsettling effect on her whenever she was near him, but it was a pleasant feeling, not one of unease or a growing need to get away. She mentally shook

77

her head. The handsome horse trainer had taken up residence in her mind since seeing him in Millie's kitchen the other day. She'd tried to stop thinking about him and their encounter in the barn for days, to no avail.

"Well, I'm glad you've returned, David. Business went well, I assume?" Lizette said next to her son.

David laughed. "Can't complain, Mother. I had a grand time in Louisville."

Emma shivered, her eyes volleying between mother and son. The icy undercurrent between the two was unmistakable, amidst their smiles and cordial words. Lizette clasped her hands together and beamed.

"Well, I've finished my breakfast. I will leave you and Emma to enjoy some time together to finally get acquainted."

Emma groaned silently. Her plans to go to the barns would have to be postponed. Something about spending time with David alone made her stomach churn.

Lizette sauntered out of the room, closing the doors behind her. Emma stood by the table, her back straight. Her palms began to sweat and she clutched her gloves tightly in her hands.

David turned fully to her, his eyes lingering on her neckline. Thankfully, her blouse had a high collar, and she fought the urge to touch her hand to her neck to check and make sure all the buttons were secured.

"I was going to see if someone could take me horseback riding and show me the estate," she said with as much cheer as she could bring forth. She stepped around him, only to be stopped by his hand reaching for her arm.

Emma glanced from his hand holding her back to his face. The urge to leave this room grew stronger. She had to get outdoors, or somewhere else, where she wasn't alone with David.

"Would you care to give me a tour, David?" Emma's

voice cracked slightly at her question. She needed to keep her composure and not allow this man to see that he'd completely intimidated her. "I've found that riding gives two people plenty of time to talk and get to know one another."

Emma stiffened. If David was going to be her husband, she would have to learn to endure his company.

"I've been on a horse most of the night to get home, my lovely Emma." David stepped closer and tugged her toward him. "I'm rather tired from the long ride." He leaned closer, his lips against her cheek.

Emma's breath caught in her throat and she leaned away from him. David's free hand came up and touched her face. His smile was a predatory leer.

"I can think of other ways we can occupy ourselves and get to know each other very well," he murmured into her ear.

Emma tugged to free herself from his grip, but he held tight. His fingers tightened around her arm. His other arm snaked around her waist and he drew her fully up against him.

"What do you say, Emma? Since my mother has planned for the wedding to be only a few weeks away, there's no reason we can't get a head start with the more pleasant aspects of marriage."

Emma opened her mouth to protest his outrageous proposal, but her words were silenced with his lips on hers. She squirmed and pressed her hands against his chest. David wouldn't budge. His lips raked across hers, the hairs from his moustache scratching the sensitive area under her nose. She raised a leg and brought her heel down on top of his foot with as much force as she could produce.

David released her instantly, a dark and angry glare in his eyes as he stepped away. He cursed and wiped a hand across his mouth.

"You are out of line, Mr. Benton," Emma panted, and backed up against the table.

David was inches in front of her again in the next instant. His hand clamped under her neck, holding her jaw and forcing her head upward. He bared his teeth as he glared down at her. The pounding in Emma's ears momentarily drowned out his words.

"You're going to learn real fast that I don't take no for an answer very often, Emma." His tone was low and threatening, whispered against her cheek. "If you're going to benefit from this union, then by damn, so will I, and I refuse to wed some unwilling prude."

He shoved her roughly away from him and turned to leave. He stopped before reaching the door and faced her again.

"Count yourself lucky that the company I've kept the last few days has kept me more than satisfied, and I am tired from the journey home. Rest assured, though, that I have a healthy appetite for female company, and since my mother bought and paid for you, I plan to take full advantage of a readily available woman in my bed." He paused, then added, "Enjoy your ride. Perhaps I'll join you later, once I've rested up a bit."

David Benton slammed the door shut on his way out of the dining room.

Emma stared after him in stunned silence. She braced her shaky arm against the table, and held one hand to her chest as if it would help to slow the erratic beating of her heart. She drew in several slow, deep breaths until her body stopped shaking.

"What have you done, Emma?" she whispered. "What have you gotten yourself into?"

She straightened and ran a finger along her sore jaw. With each passing second, the fear that David Benton had managed to elicit in her turned to anger. How dare he handle her like some cheap harlot?

That's exactly what you could have ended up being if you hadn't answered the ad, Emma.

At least she'd be well taken care of and provided for in this situation, but it was becoming clearer by the day that Lizette Benton had known exactly what she was doing when she'd picked Emma to come and marry her son. She had no other recourse but to go through with this marriage. The reason why David hadn't found a wife on his own was becoming quite apparent.

Emma straightened her shirtwaist and bent to pick up her gloves that she'd dropped while struggling to ward off David's advances. She adjusted her hat, making sure the pins were still in place, and took in a final deep breath of air.

David Benton was not going to ruin this day for her. If he thought he could intimidate her so that she'd come to his bed willingly before they were properly wed, he could think again. She wasn't going to cower. Instead, she would demand that he treat her with respect.

Emma marched from the dining room, her back straight and her shoulders squared. Judith met her by the front door.

"I'm going for a ride," she informed the maid. "Should anyone come looking for me."

"Yes'm," the maid said timidly, and opened the front door for her.

Emma moved out the door and down the steps of the portico, then headed down the path toward the barn. Her mood lifted with only a few deep breaths of the spring air infused with the smell of grass. By the time she entered the carriage house, her nerves were less frazzled and it became easier to push her encounter with David Benton to the back of her mind. If Gus could find a suitable riding horse for her, that was all she needed to make this a pleasant day..

Chapter Eleven

Sam handed the lead rope to Star, the filly he'd brought in from pasture, to Ollie.

"Get her tacked up and ready to go to the track," he said absently.

His gaze drifted to the gravel road that led from the big house to the stables. Approaching the carriage barn was Emma Waterston. She walked with her back straight and her shoulders squared, and was clearly in a hurry. The hat on her head bobbed as if it was about to tumble to the ground. Her dark hair appeared to be unbound, bouncing loosely down her back.

Sam swallowed. She was dressed to go riding, near as he could tell. Her tan skirts swirled around her legs, and her jacket hugged her feminine curves.

"I thought you said you wanted to tack her up yourself." Ollie's words drifted into his mind, sounding far away.

"Changed my mind," Sam answered. "I'll meet you at the track in fifteen minutes."

Without another glance at the exercise rider, he walked a straight path toward the barn. There was no doubt why she was here. She must have taken Millie's suggestion from the other day to find Gus when she wanted to go riding.

He entered the barn from one end, just as Emma sauntered in through the other. Emma stopped in her tracks. Her eyes widened when they fell on him. Sam cursed under his breath while the beating of his heart increased. He was behaving like some wet-nosed schoolboy, chasing the skirts of a first infatuation. He pulled his cap from his head and strode fully into the barn.

Gus sat on a wooden tack trunk, oiling a bridle. He raised his head, looking from Sam to Emma.

"Miss Emma," Gus greeted and stood. He set the bridle aside and walked up to her. "What brings you to the barns on such a fine morning?"

Emma lifted her chin and smiled at Gus.

"I was hoping you could find a horse for me to ride. Mrs. Benton told me to come and see you."

Gus chuckled. He rubbed his hand along his lower jaw. "Well, I'm sure we can find a suitable horse." He glanced toward Sam.

Sam moved closer, kicking himself for just standing there like some dumb mule. He'd better get his head out of the clouds, as Millie would say. Why had he even come here? Ollie was waiting for him with the filly he needed to work.

"Sam, you showed up just in time." Gus cleared his throat. He leaned forward and rubbed at his lower back. He groaned dramatically. "My rheumatism is acting up again. I don't think I can saddle a horse today. You should pick out a riding horse for Miss Emma and give her a tour of the place."

"I've got horses to train," Sam shot back quickly. He narrowed his eyes on Gus. The old man had been perfectly fine earlier and hadn't complained about his rheumatism.

"Nonsense." Gus waved him off. "You already worked Dusty, and Ollie can handle things for an hour or so."

Emma moved closer, her soft eyes on him. "I just need someone to get me a suitable horse. I can tack it up myself, if need be. I've done it before. I don't want to take up any of your time."

The pleading look in her eyes was too much. Sam clenched his jaw, shot a hasty look at Gus, then nodded to

84

her.

"If you don't mind waiting while I finish up with a filly I've got to work, I'll find you a horse."

Emma's face purely glowed when she smiled and nodded enthusiastically.

"And find a horse for yourself, too," Gus chimed in. "You can't let the lady go riding off by herself. She doesn't know the grounds."

Emma quickly shook her head. "Oh, no, I couldn't impose like that. Someone else can escort me."

"Nonsense." Gus waved her off. "Sam'll be happy to show you around, ain't that right, Sam?" Without waiting for an answer, he continued. "Why, just last night he told me it would be good for one of his young horses – I forgot the animal's name - to go out with one of the older ones, and learn not to be so skittish. This is a good opportunity for that."

Sam glared at his mentor. Gus had him cornered like a rat in a barn full of cats.

"I suppose that would be a good idea," he said slowly.

What the hell was he getting himself into now? If Emma was going to go riding, someone needed to escort her, just in case something happened. Her horse could spook and throw her, or she could even get lost. It was a bad idea for him to be her escort, for more reasons than he could think of at the moment.

Sam looked at her. "I'll be about a half hour with the horse I've got working on the track. You can wait here with Gus until I'm finished." He turned to leave. Maybe she'd change her mind, if she had to wait long enough.

Emma rushed up beside him. "Would you mind if I come and watch?"

Sam tilted his head to the side to look at her next to him. "I suppose you can watch," he grumbled.

The subtle scent of her perfume drifted to his nose,

and her hair bounced down her back. He'd only seen her with her hair pinned up, and an irrational urge to run his fingers through her strands made him tighten his hands into a fist. This insane attraction for a woman who belonged to someone else was going to drive him mad.

It was one thing if she'd stay as invisible as Mrs. Benton, and only lived in his mind, but to have her be here, spending time at the stables with the horses where he had to see and talk to her, might be too much. The knowledge that she belonged to that bastard made his pulse pound in his head.

"I've always loved watching horses run in the fields," she said, reining in his thoughts. "And I've been to the races at Saratoga and Baltimore, but I've never been this close to racehorses."

Sam glanced at her out of the corner of his eye. "They're beautiful animals, but also powerful and unpredictable sometimes, especially the young ones."

She raised her head to look at him. "How is your shoulder?"

Sam rubbed at the injury.

"Much better. I don't know what kind of magic Millie puts in her concoctions, but she sure knows how to ease aches and pains."

Emma laughed softly. Sam groaned in silence.

"I bet her secret ingredient is bourbon. It's what she uses religiously in her cooking."

Sam chuckled. "I wouldn't doubt it."

Their eyes met and something squeezed tightly around Sam's heart. Emma's smile was radiant and genuine, making her eyes shine warmly. How easy it was to talk to her, compared to their first encounter in the mare barn. She was different today, more relaxed and less formal. Looking past her expensive outfit, it was easy to think of her as someone other than a blueblood.

Ollie had Star jogging down the dirt track when Sam approached. He leaned his forearms on the low wooden railing, his gaze focused on the horse and how she moved. She'd been slightly off a week ago, and if she was trying to come up lame, it was best to see it before it happened.

"Let her lope for a half mile, and see how she feels," he called to Ollie. The rider nodded, indicated that he'd heard.

"Beautiful," Emma whispered next to him.

Sam couldn't agree more, but he wasn't thinking about the horse. He moved away from the railing and onto the track, just to put some distance between himself and Emma. How was he going to spend an hour or more with her, showing her around the farm?

He'd heard the grooms talk about their infatuations with women, and some of them had claimed to have fallen in love with someone at first sight, without even knowing them. No one had ever mentioned falling for a woman who was spoken for by another man, or who fell outside their social ranks.

Ollie eased Star to a stop in front of him, and Sam blinked. He hadn't even paid attention to the filly.

"How'd she feel?" he asked. "I didn't see anything wrong with her."

"No, she seems sound," Ollie confirmed. His eyes drifted to the fence for a second before he shot Sam a quizzical look.

"I'm going to take Miss Waterston for a ride and show her the estate. Cool Star out and wrap her front legs. Best to put her in a stall and we'll see how she is tomorrow. I want to make sure I don't miss anything."

Ollie's eyes widened, but he nodded.

"Sure, Sam."

No doubt, Ollie wanted to say a lot more. He hopped from the filly's back while Sam held the bridle. He lingered on the horse's left side, where Emma couldn't see him.

"Never thought I'd see the day where you mingle with the bluebloods," he whispered, and took the reins from Sam.

Sam shrugged. "She's different," he said, almost gruffly.

"Whatever you say." Ollie led the filly from the track.

"Tell Ben or one of the other grooms to saddle Ace for me," Sam said in a normal tone. Ollie's brows shot up, but he didn't say anything.

"What a magnificent animal," Emma said, looking at the filly with awestruck eyes as Ollie led her away.

Sam came up beside her. "I'll show you Dusty sometime. Then you'll have seen a magnificent horse."

"I'd like that," she nodded and dropped her gaze as if she'd said something she shouldn't have. Clearly, she was struggling with the social boundaries her kind imposed.

Sam led her to the barn that housed the saddle horses. David Benton's gelding was there. Sam frowned. When had Benton returned? And if he was home, why was Emma at the stables, rather than at the house with him? He mentally shook his head. It was none of his business.

"Is Dusty the one who injured your arm?" she asked when he stopped in front of one of the stalls.

"Yeah, he's the one that got me," he confirmed. Sam lifted the halter from the peg on the wall and opened the stall door. "It wasn't his fault. He's young and full of energy."

"Is this the horse I'll be riding?" Emma was right behind him. "He looks almost like my Ajax."

Sam put the halter on the gentle gelding, which had dutifully lowered its head.

"Meet Whiskey," he said. "Your riding mount for

today."

Emma laughed. "Does everything in Kentucky revolve around alcohol?"

Sam glanced her way just as her face turned serious as if she'd said something bad. A fleeting look of annoyance passed through her eyes like she'd realized something with her question.

"Not always," Sam said lightly. "But we do like our fast horses and bourbon."

Her mouth tightened and a hard, almost painful and panicked stare passed through her eyes. "I'm beginning to realize that," she murmured.

Sam stepped toward her. He lifted his arm, but stopped himself just in time before touching her; comforting her. He turned back to the horse, looping the lead rope through the tie ring on the wall by his stall. He cursed David Benton to hell. There was only one reason she had that look in her eyes. Obviously, she'd had the unpleasant experience of facing her fiancé while he was drunk.

He cleared his throat. An employee didn't get mixed up with the affairs of the big house.

"Let me get this horse groomed and saddled, then I'll fetch my own mount so we can get going," he said, keeping his voice even.

"I'll groom him," Emma said quickly. She stared up at him. "Please. I don't mind. I've always found it soothing to brush Ajax."

Sam's eyes locked with hers. "You couldn't have your horse shipped to Kentucky?"

Emma gave a soft laugh. "I don't have him anymore. My father sold him years ago."

Abruptly, she turned away from him and rummaged through the wooden trunk. Sam gritted his teeth. Instead of cheering her up, he'd clearly upset her. The bitterness

89

in her voice was laced with deep-rooted pain.

Keep your distance, Hawley.

There was so much to ask her. Foremost on his mind was the reason Emma would consent to a marriage to David Benton. Instead of opening his mouth to ask, he gave her some space. He fetched a sidesaddle that hadn't seen use in ages and bridle from the tack room.

By the time Whiskey was tacked up, Emma smiled again. She stepped up to the horse and pulled the stirrup down the saddle. She reached for the pommel then glanced over her shoulder.

Sam stepped up to her, bent forward and hooked his hands together for her foot so he could give her a lift. He stood so close behind her, her hair tickled his nose, and he inhaled the soft fragrance of her perfume.

You're treading a dangerous line, Hawley.

Sam's gaze locked with hers and a ripple of longing spread through him. Her eyes widened for a fraction of a second, and the emotion he read there mirrored his own reaction, sending another dose of awareness through him. She quickly averted her gaze and pulled herself into the saddle, adjusting her skirt over her legs. Sam supported her longer than necessary.

She'd barely seated herself in the saddle, when Ollie came charging into the barn, breathing hard.

"Sam, you're gonna want to come. Quick."

Sam's eyes shot to Emma, then to his frantic-looking groom.

"What's going on?" he demanded, his insides still alive from his reaction to touching Emma.

"There's big trouble at the mare barn."

Chapter Twelve

"I apologize, Emma. I know you were looking forward to this ride."

Sam's words were spoken with such sincerity, they seemed to reach straight inside her and wrap around her heart.

"The ride can wait." Emma offered a smile.

He nodded, regret in his eyes. "Get Whiskey back to his stall, Ollie," he said to the groom, whose wide eyes darted between them.

Sam raised his arms, his hands at her waist to support her dismount, and Emma scrambled from Whiskey's back. His secure hold lingered when her feet touched the ground.

"Go," she said and maneuvered away from him. His touch was too unsettling. Not in a bad way, like David's touch had made her feel. Sam's touch was more than pleasant, and the feeling was disturbing.

His eyes connected with hers for another second before he sprinted from the barn. Emma smiled at the groom, to whom she handed Whiskey's reins. He nodded politely, then quickly averted his gaze and led the gelding back to his stall.

Emma sighed. What to do now? She could easily tell Ollie not to untack the horse and simply ride out on her own, but something compelled her to follow Sam. From the moment he'd walked into the carriage barn earlier, her heart had started to beat faster than usual.

He wasn't the rude man she'd first assumed. He seemed closed off and tense in her company, but could she blame him? The first time they'd met in the mare barn, she'd certainly told him that he was beneath her. He'd turned out to be far more pleasant company than the man she was going to marry in a few short weeks.

An icy chill spilled down her back. David Benton made her feel as if she was nothing but an acquisition; something bought and paid for.

In a way, that's what you are, Emma.

David may not have sent for her, but his mother certainly had. She'd paid her well in beautiful dresses and other fineries, along with the promise of a life of wealth. This was her opportunity to pretend she was the woman she'd been years ago in Boston.

Emma quietly shook her head. She was no longer that woman. She'd realized it more and more with each day that passed since coming here. She preferred the company of the cook, or Gus at the stables, to Lizette Benton. Her gaze drifted to where Sam had disappeared through the wide barn doors.

Her hands smoothed down the front of her riding habit, drifting to her waist where the pleasant feel of Sam's strong hands still lingered. She preferred his company, and his touch, to that of the man she was going to marry. Never before had two men elicited such strong, but opposite feelings in her.

Emma walked out of the barn. Loud men's voices came from the mare barn. She lengthened her strides, and her forehead wrinkled. What was going on? As she drew closer, a jolt of dread rushed through her, making her limbs go weak. One of those voices belonged to David, her fiancé. The other one was Sam's, and there was also Gus' voice, but it was much calmer.

"Get the hell out of my way, Hawley," David roared.

Emma ran into the barn. Sam stood in front of a stall, the same stall that housed the mare she'd petted the first time she'd come to the stables. He was clearly blocking David's way. Her fiancé held a rifle in his hand. Emma's eyes widened.

"Over my dead body," Sam growled. "You're not getting near this mare." The anger and animosity in his eyes as he stared down David Benton was clear to see, even from a distance.

"That can easily be arranged," David retorted. "You're overstepping your place here, and I'll have you removed for insubordination. It's been long overdue."

"Mr. Benton," Gus said, holding out his hand and stepping closer to the enraged man. "Your mother wouldn't want you to act in the heat of the moment."

David shot an angry glare at the old caretaker. Several grooms stood around, watching the scene unfold.

"I don't give a damn about what my mother would want me to do," David slurred. He took a step toward Gus, raising the gun in a threatening gesture which was clearly meant to intimidate. "My mother won't be in charge of this estate much longer."

Emma rushed down the barn aisle.

"What in heaven's name is going on here?" she implored, trying to sound like her own mother used to sound when she'd caught Emma doing something she'd deemed unladylike.

All eyes snapped to her. Emma focused her gaze on her fiancé, not at the man who guarded the stall, staring at her with disbelief on his face.

"Miss Emma, I don't think you should be here," Gus said quickly, trying to ward her off.

"I'd like to know what three grown men are doing in this barn, acting like a bunch of fighting little boys," she said with as much force to her voice as she could muster. She cleared her throat, her heart pounding in her chest. She had no authority to be here and make such demands, but hopefully she could diffuse the tense situation enough to calm everyone down.

"So, my lovely bride has some spunk after all." David

laughed as he lowered the rifle. He moved around Gus and stood in front of her. He leaned forward. "And here I thought you were a passionless, empty shell, Emma."

The stench of bourbon wafted from his mouth. He must have bathed in a barrel of liquor for him to be this inebriated in such a short amount of time. She hadn't left the house more than an hour ago. Emma stared up at him. He was not going to intimidate her again.

"I thought you were too tired to go riding earlier," she challenged. "Yet I see you're not too tired to drink, and make a fool of yourself in front of your staff," she hissed under her breath. No doubt her words carried to the other men.

David's lips twitched and he almost bared his teeth. "Watch your place, Emma. You may be the future mistress here, but that doesn't give you the right to issue orders, especially to me."

Emma straightened and backed up a step. "I demand to know why you're pointing a rifle at Sam Hawley."

David laughed scornfully. "Sam Hawley, is it? Is he the one you were meeting to take you for a ride? I wasn't good enough?"

Emma's mouth opened. Her arm came up before she had time to think about her actions. With a resounding smack, her hand connected with her fiancé's cheek.

"How dare you make such insinuations," she hissed. "You're the one who told me to go, that you were too tired to take me horseback riding."

David's eyes widened and he held his own hand to his cheek, then grabbed for her. In the same instant, Sam rushed forward and yanked David's rifle from his grip, tossing it to Gus before putting himself between Emma and her enraged fiancé.

"You need to go and sleep off the alcohol, Benton, before you do something rash. Like Gus said, your mother isn't going to be happy when she hears what you're planning to do."

His back was to Emma, but every muscle visibly tensed beneath Sam's shirt. David stood a good inch taller than Sam, but he wasn't as broad or solidly built. No doubt David hadn't done much physical work in his life.

"I'll escort you back to the house, Mr. Benton," Gus said calmly. "Some rest, and we can discuss this a little more civilly, and make a decision on what to do about the mare."

Emma stepped around Sam to look at David.

"I still don't know what's going on." Her eyes volleyed between the two men.

Sam turned to her. "Queen foaled a stillborn, just like last year."

"The mare is useless. She's an expense we don't need if she can't produce," David slurred.

Sam leaned forward, his face inches from David's. "If you had listened to what Gus and everyone else told you last year, and not insisted she be bred again so soon, this might not have happened. She's given this farm eight excellent foals over the past nine years. Her body needs a rest."

The two men stared at each other, hatred gleaming in both their eyes. Emma held her breath. A physical fight between them could break out at any second. She touched her hand to David's arm and smiled up at him when he shot her a startled look. If this argument turned violent, Sam could well lose his job.

"Please don't do this, David," she implored. "Return to the house with me, and I'll ask Millie to brew you some coffee or whatever else you'd like."

She cringed when he leered at her. Gus tugged on Sam's arm and he backed away. David swayed slightly, then yanked his arm from her hand. He glared at Sam.

"This isn't over, Hawley," he threatened, then pushed his way past Gus and staggered out of the barn alone.

Gus glanced from Sam to Emma, then hobbled as fast as he could after the inebriated man.

Emma breathed a sigh of relief. Her eye caught Sam's stare. He looked at her as if she'd sprouted horns and a tail. Around them, the grooms who had witnessed the scene all murmured at once. Sam raised his head.

"Get back to your jobs," he ordered and they dispersed, leaving the barn empty and quiet again.

Sam ran a hand through his hair. He paced in front of the mare's stall, not looking at Emma. Finally, he stopped and raised his head to her.

"What do you see in that bastard to come all the way from Boston to marry him?" His chin jutted down the barn aisle in the direction David had gone.

Emma stiffened at the forward question. There was an almost pleading look in Sam's blue eyes, which were filled with longing. She dropped eye contact as her heart sped up. Why couldn't this man be the one she had come to marry? David Benton didn't deserve all of his wealth and privileges.

She raised her chin when he continued to look at her, waiting for an answer. Inhaling deeply, she blew the air slowly from her mouth. Did it matter if he knew the truth about her? That she wasn't the wealthy lady he and, no doubt everyone else, thought she was? She'd already confided in Millie.

"Lizette Benton placed an ad for a wife in a paper called the Grooms' Gazette."

Sam's forehead wrinkled, and he shook his head slightly. He stepped up to her, his gaze roaming over her face. Emma's limbs weakened in reaction to his perusal.

"I'm a mail order bride," she continued in a soft whisper. "I had no other choice but to find a husband or I would have been out on the street." She laughed softly. "The more I see of David Benton, the more I understand why Lizette would go through such extremes to find her son a wife."

"Lizette Benton is too much of a blueblood to do something like that," Sam said slowly. His eyes were still filled with incomprehension. "She believes in pure bloodlines, in her horses as well as in people."

Emma nodded. "I come from a wealthy family. I was raised in Boston's elite society. My father liked to gamble, and unbeknownst to my mother, lost most of her money in various business deals that failed. When she died, the creditors came and took what was left. My father moved on, and I was left to my own devices."

Sam's hand reached up, hesitated, then touched her arm, giving it a gentle squeeze. Her body's reaction to his touch was instant. The air left her lungs and a warm feeling rushed through her limbs. She licked at her lips and stared up into his sincere eyes.

"I'm sorry," he said, clearly at a loss for words.

Emma swallowed past the growing lump in her throat. "Through a friend of the family, I found work at a textile mill in Lawrence. For the last year, that's where I worked, until the factory burned down. One by one, my friends moved on, taking the advice of others to find husbands." She laughed again. "Of the four of us who lived together, I was the last one to give in. When I saw the ad David's mother had placed in his name, I thought my prayers had been answered, and I could go back to the life I had before."

A flash of annoyance passed through Sam's eyes. He dropped his hand from her arm and stepped away.

"You're going to go through with this marriage?" he asked, almost angrily.

"I have no choice, Sam. I don't have a penny to my

name, and Lizette made it clear to me that I would be on my own if I didn't marry David."

He was in front of her again in the next instant. "You don't have to marry him," he nearly growled.

Emma avoided eye contact. She stepped away from him when he reached for her again.

"I have to go," she stammered.

Her legs were as heavy as lead when she rushed from the barn. Her feelings for Sam Hawley scared her more than anything ever had, and she had to get away. What she'd read in his eyes could never be. How could he show such tender feelings for her, not even knowing her? And likewise, how was it possible that she'd been so instantly attracted to him, from the moment she'd first seen him at the train station?

Emma raced up the stairs to her room and leaned against her closed door. She held her hand over her pounding heart and squeezed her eyes shut. Right now, she needed the advice of her friends, but they were too far away. She spoke each of their names out loud and laughed bitterly.

"Willow. Rose. Gillian. Is it possible to fall in love with someone at first sight?"

Chapter Thirteen

Emma's heart pounded when she slipped from her room and descended the stairs, intent to head for the kitchen. She hadn't left her chambers since the incident at the barn earlier today. She'd spent the rest of the morning and well into the afternoon staring out the balcony window, thinking about a man who shouldn't be in her thoughts.

All her life, she'd watched her parents in a loveless marriage. Her mother had always told her that marriages were for convenience. It was a mutual partnership where both parties gained something. Emma had always been at a loss about what her mother had gained from her father, because he seemed to have benefitted the most from their marriage. He'd spent Mother's wealth freely.

Giving her heart to a man had never been an option. That's why it hadn't been difficult to come to Kentucky. Marrying David would provide her with a home of luxury. In exchange, she'd grace his arm in public. Lizette had hinted at children during one of their conversations, and Emma had accepted that part of the marriage arrangement, although the thought of being intimate with David made her stomach churn.

Never had she expected to find a man who could make her pulse quicken with a simple smile, or her skin tingle with a soft touch. She shook her head. She had to stop thinking about Sam Hawley. They were two people who were worlds apart. He would never fit into polite society.

You've lived in his world, Emma.

Did she want to go back to that? Could she? A life of poverty, always struggling to make ends meet. Sam wasn't exactly poor. He had a secure position here at the Three Elms and a roof over his head. The near-fight between him and David flashed before her eyes.

David could easily terminate Sam's employment. As an employee, he'd crossed the line, no matter the reason. Emma had been appalled to hear that David wanted to shoot the mare simply because she hadn't produced a live foal. How could someone have so little regard for another living being?

She scoffed. David didn't seem to regard anything or anyone, other than himself. She'd heard shouting earlier between him and Lizette, but she hadn't dared leave her room. Even when Judith, the maid, had knocked on her door to let her know that supper was being served, she'd feigned a stomachache and said she was already in bed.

She had no desire for another confrontation with her fiancé today. Perhaps by morning, he would be more reasonable again. Hopefully his mother and Gus, or whoever was overseer of the horse operation, had talked some sense into David, and the mare would be safe. It had been clear that he hadn't thought his actions through. Who in their right mind would simply shoot an animal in the heat of the moment?

Emma sighed and tiptoed down the final steps of the staircase. She glanced in both directions of the great entrance hall, then headed for the kitchen. Millie was the person with whom she needed to speak. The cook was the closest she had to a true friend here, and she trusted her to keep things confidential. Would it be wise to tell her about Sam, and her feelings for him? What good would it do? In a couple of weeks she was going to marry David.

The kitchen was eerily quiet when she entered. The strong aroma of baked goods drifted through the air, making Emma's mouth water. She hadn't eaten all day. Several loaves of bread lined a section of the workbench, and one had already been cut. Emma helped herself to a slice and glanced around the galley. The kitchen was spotless, as always. Pots and pans hung from the ceiling, and the stove was clean, without a trace of soot anywhere.

Emma swallowed the last of the bread. She glanced toward the servants' entrance, then to the corridor that led to Millie's bedroom. She wouldn't have retired this early. Perhaps Millie had gone to visit Gus, even though it was already getting dark outside.

A smile passed over her face. The old caretaker and the outspoken cook cared for each other. Everyone knew it and talked about it, except for those two stubborn old people. They both needed a good nudge in the rear to get them together.

Emma headed for the servants' door leading outside. A stroll in the fresh air might do her some good and help clear her jumbled mind. All was quiet and peaceful in the early evening, the final glow of the day disappearing in an orange and red hue into the horizon, giving itself over to the night. Stars already twinkled in the sky, and Emma tilted her head back to see.

She wrapped her arms around her middle and shivered slightly at the cool breeze. She'd forgotten a shawl, but hadn't expected to come outside at this late hour. Off in the distance, a horse whinnied and another answered its call. She smiled. Everything seemed so peaceful here, and quiet. It was so unlike the loud noises in the city. Except for the man she'd come here to marry, Kentucky was perfect.

Emma walked down the lane, guided by the feel of gravel beneath her feet. The glow from the house gave her a little light by which to see and it wasn't completely dark yet. The barns and horses called to her, drawing her closer to them and further away from the life she'd imagined she wanted. Calling to her was a different life, and a man who was so unlike any other. Being in his company would lead to scandal from which she could never recover. Yet, why didn't it seem to matter?

Emma stopped just before she reached one of several outbuildings. She turned to look back at the large, white house. It stood tall and imposing against the darkening skies, with all its grandeur. Was she willing to give up her life of luxury?

Gillian's message to her in her letter came to mind.

If you find a man half as good as Rhys, then you will find a wealth far beyond that of money.

Had she found such a man in Sam Hawley? She laughed. This was ridiculous. What would she even say to him? He had an obvious dislike for the wealthy. She'd seen something in his eyes earlier today; some emotion that both exhilarated and frightened her, but it had quickly vanished when she'd said she'd come here to marry for money. No doubt he thought of her as being no different than David or Lizette Benton.

The scrunching sound of shoes on gravel reached her ear, and she glanced around. A quick gasp escaped her mouth when a man's shadow materialized.

"Sneaking off to visit a filthy stable hand is not becoming of a lady, Emma."

David's lecherous voice sent her heart to racing. She darted a quick look at the house, judging the distance to get back.

"I was out here for some fresh air, nothing more," she said with as much force as she could produce. Her throat tightened painfully. "I don't appreciate your improper inferences, David," she added for good measure.

He stood in front of her in the next instant and grabbed her arm, his fingers biting painfully into her skin. Yanking her closer, his breath was hot against her cheek.

"I don't take kindly to someone making a fool of me

in front of my employees, least of all a female who's using her charms to impress the hired help."

Emma sucked in a quick breath of air. "I was doing no such thing, David." She leaned away from him. "You made a fool of yourself all on your own."

David tugged on her arm, his grip tightening. Emma fought back, digging her shoes into the gravel.

"Release me this instant," she demanded.

David grabbed her more forcefully, dragging her toward one of the sheds.

"I will not have some female make me the laughingstock here," he growled. "My mother orders me around enough. It's time you learned your place here, Emma. If you want to reap the bounty of being my wife, you're going to have to earn it."

"What are you talking about?" she stammered. A chill raced through her at his words. She struggled against him, her hand on his, trying to unclamp his fingers from her arm.

"I shouldn't have been so soft with you this morning, my sweet Emma. No woman's ever refused me, and I expect the one I marry to be available for me when I demand it."

"Let me go, David." Emma's heart pounded in her ears and her limbs weakened with panic.

David pulled the door open to one of the outbuildings and pushed her inside. She stumbled and fell onto hard earth. She scrambled to her feet, but before she'd completely regained a foothold, the back of David's hand connected with her cheek, sending her against the wall. Emma gasped from the impact.

"You will learn your place here, and I will not tolerate you fraternizing with the stable help," he roared. Before she had a chance to move away, David reached for her again, ripping at the bodice of her dress.

103

"Don't do this, David," she breathed, fear consuming her.

She clawed at his arms and face, but he was stronger. He pinned her arms to her sides and her back against the wall. She kicked up with her knee, catching David near his groin. He cursed loudly, then backhanded her again with such force, the back of her head crashed against the wooden slats of the wall with a loud thump.

* * *

Sam leaned over Queen's stall. She munched on some hay in the corner and seemed settled enough. He hadn't been around when she'd gone into labor. Ollie had run to get him when he was about to take Emma Waterston for a ride. That was the first time he had heard that the mare had dropped another stillborn. Anger coursed through him again, thinking about what had happened.

He'd been ready to kill David Benton when he'd seen him with a rifle in his hand. No doubt he'd been trying to make a point to his mother that he wanted to be in charge. Everyone knew that Lizette controlled the business end of the farm, even if she pretended to let her son be in charge.

Emma had surprised the hell out of him, the way she'd stood up to Benton. Sam ran a hand over his face. He hadn't been able to think of anything else all day. Something had happened to him this morning. He'd been infatuated with her since the first time he saw her, but seeing her defending the mare, he'd fallen in love.

When she'd told him about why she was here as Benton's bride, he'd wanted to take her in his arms and tell her to marry him instead. He'd been stopped cold by her words, that she'd wanted to return to the kind of life she'd had in Boston. How could she choose to sell herself to a bastard like Benton? She wanted her life of privilege. It's what she'd said. She wouldn't settle for someone like him, a mere horse trainer.

If she really only cared about money, then she and Benton deserved each other. Something told him, however, that she wasn't sure what she wanted. What classy lady spent time at the barns with the stable hands, or in the kitchen with the cook? Emma may have grown up among the elite, but her year away from high society had changed her. She may think it's what she wanted, but maybe he could show her that there was much more to living than having money.

Sam pushed away from the stall and headed up the barn aisle. The sky outside was getting darker, but he wasn't ready to go back to the cottage yet. Millie and Gus had gone to visit a mutual friend at a neighboring farm and wouldn't be back until morning. Being alone in the house would only make him more restless.

Sam stood just outside the barn and stared up at the sky. The tranquil sounds of horses rustling in their stalls behind him should give him some peace. Every muscle in his body was taut, however. David Benton had been spoiled all his life, and Lizette had to clean up his messes. Now she was trying to clean up his image by ordering him a pretty wife, as if Emma was some trinket to appease her son.

Sam's jaw twitched uncontrollably. He stared toward the big house. Lights shone through the trees, beckoning to him. Minutes later, he was walking up the path leading toward those lights. He cursed under his breath.

What do you think's gonna happen, Hawley? That she'll be standing there, waiting for you?

A dull thud drew his head around. The sound came from one of the equipment sheds. A second later, the sound repeated, followed by a female's weak voice. A

105

sensation flowed through him as if someone had dumped a bucket of ice water over him. Sam ran toward the sound of the voice. He yanked open the squeaky door to the shed, widening his eyes to the darkness. The silhouettes of two figures came into view. A man towered over a woman, who moaned quietly.

Sam rushed up to the man. The faint odor of bourbon drifted to his nose. When he grabbed for the man's shirt, the handful of expensive material in his fingers left no doubt of his identity. Sam hauled David Benton away from the woman and threw him against the opposite wall.

"Help me." A weak plea reached him from out of the darkness.

Another surge of anger turned Sam's blood to boiling. Emma? How had she ended up in this shed with Benton? He had no time to help her. The man came at him, sending a fist against his jaw. Sam took the blow and delivered one of his own.

Rage took over. He lunged at Benton, sending them both crashing against the wall. His shirt tore when Benton grabbed at him. Again and again, he swung at the man he'd loathed since they were boys. They wrestled on the ground, then ended up outside somehow. Benton managed to get to his feet at the same time Sam stood. Sam advanced on him again, but Emma's quiet call from inside stopped him. What had the bastard done to her?

"You're going to regret this, Hawley," Benton panted, then backed away into the darkness.

Sam rushed into the shed.

"Emma?"

He dropped to his knees beside her, feeling for her. His fingers made contact with bare skin below her neck. The front of her dress was torn. In the darkness, it was impossible to see how much of her was exposed, but it

106

was best not to find out. He stripped his coat down his arms and wrapped it around her, lifting her head.

"Emma?" he called again, and touched her cheek.

A soft groan was his answer. "Sam," she barely whispered.

Sam lifted her into his arms, ignoring the dull pain that lingered in his shoulder from his healing injury. As fast as his legs would move, he carried her to his cottage.

Chapter Fourteen

Sam sat at the small table in the kitchen, clutching a hot cup of coffee between his hands. His elbows rested heavily on the grainy wood. He stared out the window, where the sun was slowly rising to give way to a new day. Any other morning, he'd be out with the horses already. Not today.

His jaw clenched tight and his gaze drifted to the door leading to his bedroom. His shoulder ached, not just the injured one, but the good side, too. He hadn't relaxed all night, his muscles strung tighter than a young racehorse eager to run. He'd never wanted to do harm to anyone the way he'd wanted to hurt David Benton last night, and still wanted to hurt him some more today.

He'd carried Emma to the cottage last night, and had lowered her into his bed, afraid to ask her how badly she was injured. Her eyes had been filled with fear, but she'd clung to him, sobbing against his chest, and he'd simply held her until she'd cried herself to sleep.

When she'd finally relaxed, he'd covered her with a blanket, his coat still draped around her. He'd spent a restless night in the front room, conjuring up all sorts of thoughts of what he would do to Benton the next time he saw him.

"Sam."

Sam bolted to his feet at the softly spoken sound of his name, the chair legs scraping against the wooden floor. His coffee spilled over the side of the cup, scalding his hand. Sam wiped the hot liquid on his pants and turned toward his bedroom. Emma stood under the door, her hair hanging in a disheveled mess around her face.

Sam stopped in front of her, just staring. There was nothing he could say to her at the moment to take away the confusion and pain in her eyes. She clutched his coat around her shoulders and returned his stare. The soft, grateful smile that hesitantly spread across her face melted his heart.

"Thank you," she whispered. "For what you did last night."

Sam swallowed. He glanced down at his hands, then back at her. "Emma, I'm sorry that bast . . . that he hurt you."

She shook her head and raised her hand to the back of her head. "The pain in my head where he knocked me against the wall will go away. I've known that David is short-tempered, but I never thought he'd turn violent and do what he tried to do."

"Tried?" Sam reached for Emma's hand. Hope sprang to life in him. Had he gotten to her in time, before Benton violated her?

Emma nodded. She clutched Sam's hand. "You came, and saved me before . . . before he had the chance to—" She broke off. There was no need for her to say the rest.

He gripped her small hand in his, consumed with the urge to pull her to him, wrap her in his arms, and tell her he'd always protect her. He broke eye contact and glanced over his shoulder into the kitchen.

"Would you like something to eat or drink? I've got coffee."

Hell. She probably didn't drink coffee.

"A cup of coffee sounds lovely." Her smile widened.

He moved aside for her to pass and move fully into the room. Sam pulled out a chair for her to sit, then poured a mug of the hot brew for her.

"I'll take sugar if you have it."

Sam set the mug, along with a spoon and a crock of sugar, in front of her.

"Gus has a sweet tooth." He grinned. "He uses sugar

in everything."

Emma laughed softly. "No wonder he enjoys Millie's baking."

Sam sat across from her and sipped at his own coffee. The small talk was killing him. There was no delicate way to approach last evening's incident, and ask her what she planned to do now. Surely, she wasn't going to go through with marrying David?

"You risked a lot for me, Sam." Emma stared at him from across the table. She spooned sugar into her coffee, then leaned forward. "Lizette is going to know about this. I will tell her what her son tried to do, and that you came to my aid. Your position here will not be compromised."

Sam straightened. She was worried about his job? She ought to be more worried about her reputation. She'd just spent the night in the cottage of a stable employee. That didn't look good in anyone's eyes, no matter what the truth was.

"Benton had it coming to him for a long time," he said gruffly. "I enjoyed every punch I threw at him." He leaned forward and stared her in the eyes. "I'd do it again in a heartbeat to keep you safe."

Emma's eyes widened. Confusion marred her pretty face. The look in her soft gaze was filled with an emotion Sam had only dreamt about.

"I've never met a man like you, Sam Hawley," she whispered, and reached across the table. He met her halfway with his hand. She grazed her fingers across the raw skin of his knuckles.

"And I've never met a lady quite like you, Emma Waterston."

His lips widened in a tentative grin.

She averted her gaze, but the faint smile that drifted across her face before she lowered her head sent a surge of awareness through him. He had to tell her that he cared for her; that he loved her. He gave her hand a squeeze and opened his mouth to speak. A knock at the door killed the mood. Emma jerked her hand away and straightened. Her eyes widened, clouded with worry.

Sam stood. The knock came again, louder this time.

"I'm coming," he grumbled.

He pulled the door open. His eyes narrowed to hide his surprise. Standing in front of him, looking like an enraged polecat, was Lizette Benton. Right next to her stood her son, a smug sneer on his face. Sam glanced from Mrs. Benton to David and smiled at the discoloration around the taller man's eye and along his jaw.

"What have you done with Miss Waterston?" Mrs. Benton demanded. "I should send for the authorities to have you arrested."

Sam stood taller, blocking the door to his home.

"Pack your bags, Hawley," David chimed in. "You're finished here."

Lizette Benton shot a warning stare at her son before turning back to Sam.

"Where is she?" she demanded. "If you've ruined her, I will have you thrown in jail for the rest of your life."

Sam smirked. "Ruined her?" He stared from her to David. "I gave her a safe place to rest for the night. What do you call it when your son violates a lady, Mrs. Benton? I came along just in time to prevent that from happening. Or is that something that is acceptable in your social circles?"

Lizette Benton's mouth widened in apparent shock. "Those are some strong insinuations. David told me you attacked him while he was taking his fiancé for a walk."

Sam couldn't keep from laughing. "Maybe you ought to ask Miss Waterston what she has to say about that, and let her tell you the real story."

"Where is she?" Mrs. Benton implored.

"I'm right here, Lizette."

Sam glanced over his shoulder, frowning. Emma walked up behind him, tightly clutching his coat around herself. She held her chin high and looked directly at Mrs. Benton, whose eyes widened even more.

"I hope you realize what this looks like, Emma," the woman implored, her piercing stare going from her to Sam. "Come along, so I can do some damage control before it's too late."

She took a step forward. Sam blocked her entrance to his home. He didn't flinch at her demanding stare. It was Emma's soft hand on his arm that made him move aside. She stepped up to Lizette and met the woman's eyes for several seconds. Slowly, she lifted aside the coat she'd clutched around herself. Mrs. Benton gasped, her eyes flying to Sam with a murderous gleam.

"Cover yourself, Emma," the woman demanded, her outraged eyes still on Sam.

Sam didn't flinch. Standing slightly behind Emma, his view of her was cut off. Not that he wanted to see what David had done to her dress before he'd pulled him away. Renewed anger boiled to the surface.

"You are correct, Lizette," Emma said slowly. "Damage control needs to be done in order to protect Sam Hawley from any accusations of wrong-doing." She raised her eyes to David, whose ogling gaze hadn't diminished. Sam clenched his fists at his side.

"What are you talking about, Emma?" Lizette's voice rose several octaves.

"I think you know very well what I'm talking about," Emma shot back without hesitation. "David, your son, did this to me. If not for Mr. Hawley, I would have been violated in the worst possible way last night."

Lizette shot a hasty glance at her son, then back to

Emma, her lips tight.

"May we come in?" she asked, her voice sounding less demanding.

Emma wrapped the coat fully around herself again and nodded. "If it's all right with Mr. Hawley."

Sam stepped out of the way, his unwavering gaze on Mrs. Benton. "It's your property." He shrugged. "Gus and I are merely tenants." He couldn't keep the contempt out of his voice.

Lizette sauntered into the main room. Sam glared at David as he passed through the door. His mother wheeled around, looking from both Sam to Emma after Sam closed the door behind him. He stepped up behind Emma, who favored him with a grateful look.

"All right," Lizette Benton said, inhaling a dramatic breath. "Here is what is going to happen. Sam Hawley, is it?" She raised her brows to him. "I've heard some things about you, and that you're a good trainer. I understand you've got my next Derby hopeful coming along nicely."

Sam suppressed a snort. Despite the fact that Emma had said his name several time since her arrival, he was surprised Mrs. Benton had noticed. He nodded.

"You will retain your position as trainer here, on the condition that not a word will be said about this incident."

Sam's brows rose. He laughed. Emma inhaled a loud breath.

"Mrs. Benton," he said slowly. "You'll protect your son at all cost, no matter who gets hurt. Always have. Always will. This time, he hurt Miss Waterston, and could have hurt her even worse if I hadn't happened to be making the rounds at the barns. How badly is he going to hurt her next time?" He stared at David, who looked as if he was ready to lunge at him. Sam was ready if he did.

"I'm not going to sweep this under the rug."

Lizette Benton straightened, her eyes widening in

disbelief. "You will lose your position here immediately if that is how you want to play," she spat. "It will be your word against mine, and David's, and Emma's. Who do you think will side with you?"

It was Emma's turn to stand straighter. "What makes you think I'm going to keep quiet on this matter, Lizette?" she said heatedly. "David assaulted me. He hit me several times and knocked me against the wall, then tore the bodice of my dress. And that was all before Sam showed up to help me."

Sam couldn't help but smile at her, even though she couldn't see with her back to him. A warm sensation flowed through him, that she was defending him to Lizette Benton.

"Emma," Lizette nearly shouted. "You can't talk like that about the man who is going to be your husband in a few weeks."

Emma laughed. "After what he did to me last night, Lizette, I refuse to marry him."

A dark, angry cloud drifted over the woman's face. "You will be out on the street, young lady, just as we discussed, if you refuse my son. You were brought here for one purpose, and I will make sure your family name is dragged through the mud if you don't uphold our agreement."

"My family name holds no merit, Lizette. You've done your research on me. You should know that. I think the people in this county, perhaps in the entire state, know what kind of son you have. That's why you had to go all the way to Boston to find a wife for him."

Lizette's eyes drifted through the room. She looked almost composed, and smug, but her eyes glared like an ice statue. "Very well." She sighed dramatically. "If that's how you want it. You will learn not to cross me. Judith will have your belongings packed and set outside the servants' entrance in one hour." Her stare intensified and she leaned toward Emma. "The belongings that you brought with you, not the gowns and fineries I have gifted to you. You are making an enormous mistake, young lady."

"I don't think so," Emma said softly, shaking her head. "For once, I know exactly what I'm doing."

"Don't think you can take anything that I've paid for," Mrs. Benton said quickly. Apparently her only weapon against Emma was money and material possessions.

Emma shook her head. "I don't plan to, Lizette," she answered calmly. "All I need are the things I brought with me. And someday, I will repay you for the train ticket you purchased to bring me out here. In a way, I have to thank you. I would not have met a man like Sam Hawley otherwise."

Mrs. Benton stared at Sam. "As for you, I want you gone from here by nightfall, as well. You won't receive a reference from me, and will not find decent work in this state, if I can help it."

Sam nodded quietly. Her threats didn't bother him. This might be his chance to pick up and move on. His only regret was breaking the news to Gus. He'd always told the old man he'd never leave him.

"Take Miss Waterston's train fare out of my final wages, Mrs. Benton." Sam met the woman's icy stare.

"Come along, David." Lizette raised her chin and sauntered to the door.

"You'd better watch your back, Hawley," David said in a low tone as he passed him.

"I've beaten you in every fight we've had. I'm not worried," Sam said. He followed them to the door and closed it the minute David Benton stepped outside.

He stood for a second, then turned to see Emma standing in the middle of the room, looking at him with worried eyes. He took a slow step toward her, then another. His heart sped up.

"Where are you going to go?" she asked when he stopped in front of her. "I'm so sorry," she added, and her eyes began to glisten. "I didn't want you to lose your position here because of me."

Sam shrugged. He lifted his hands to her arms. "I've got friends in the area. I'm sure someone will give me a place to stay until I figure out what to do. Lizette Benton can make all the threats she wants, but she knows she's not going to win." He hesitated, then his hands slid up and down her arms along the fabric of his bulky coat. She nearly drowned inside it.

"What about you, Emma?" He stepped closer. Tears pooled in her eyes.

"I don't know," she whispered. "I'll look for work so I can buy a ticket back to Boston, I suppose. I don't want you to pay for my ticket."

His hand reached up. He hesitated for a fraction of a second, then he slid his fingers along her chin, under her hair to the back of her head, and curved around her slender neck. When he took another step closer her dress grazed his pants. He stared down at her for what seemed like an eternity.

Emma matched his stare. She swallowed visibly. Sam leaned forward. He hesitated again, then his lips touched hers. Heat coursed through him the instant his mouth came in contact with the feminine softness of her lips. She reached up, her arms curling around his neck, and she drew him closer. Sam eased back, looking for permission in the warmth of her gaze. Staring into her eyes, he communicated the promise of a future. Together.

"Emma Waterston," he murmured. "I know this is sudden, but I've offered to pay your way from Boston to Kentucky for a reason. Will you do me the honor and be my mail order bride?"

116

He touched his lips to hers again without waiting for an answer. Emma's body swayed against him, melting to him as if she'd always been meant to be in his embrace. Sam snaked his arm around her waist and drew her even closer, deepening the kiss. His fingers weaved through her hair, holding her to him, savoring every delicious second as her own mouth shifted beneath his, and he had his answer.

Chapter Fifteen

"Well, now. Maybe I need to be gone overnight more often."

Emma tensed at the voice coming from the front door, and pulled out of Sam's arms. She stumbled backward, but he caught and steadied her. A wide grin spread across his face. Emma darted a mortified glance to where Gus stood, his face beaming like a ray of sunshine.

"Or perhaps I needed to stay gone longer."

"You're home early." Sam turned to face the old man, his arm still tightly wrapped around Emma's waist.

Her cheeks heated at the smug look on the old caretaker's face.

"Saw it right from the start," Gus announced, nodding vigorously. He apparently chose to ignore Sam's comment. "Didn't know how long it would take for the two of you to realize it, too. Some things are just stronger than social boundaries."

"I wasn't going to wait as long as you, old man." Sam's eyes returned to Emma and he winked, then tugged her up against him for another kiss.

"Sam," she whispered in protest. "This isn't proper."

His brows rose, while Gus chuckled and moved further into the room.

"Now you're worried about propriety, Miss Waterston? I thought you were reformed."

Emma couldn't help but smile back at Sam, but shot him a disapproving look for good measure. Her heart filled with an emotion she hadn't thought would come alive in her. She loved Sam. There was no defining moment when it had happened.

The way he'd greeted her at the train station in Lexington replayed in her mind; his smile, her name on his lips, and the confident air around him had drawn her to him instantly. Last night, however, had solidified the feeling in her. It was like Gus had said. Some forces were simply too strong and defied logic. She'd come to Kentucky with the promise of material riches. She'd found so much more.

Emma returned Sam's smile and relaxed against him. There was nothing improper about openly showing her affection for this man. In his eyes was the promise of a future filled with love, and someone who would always take care of her. She would have a marriage filled with more wealth than she could have ever hoped.

Sam finally eased his hold around her and guided her back to the kitchen chair. He adjusted his coat around her shoulders, which had come loose and exposed too much of her torn bodice at the moment.

"I'll fetch your bag so you can change your dress," he murmured against her cheek.

Gus' keen eyes darted from her to Sam. There were untold questions in the old man's gaze. Sam poured a mug of coffee for him, and the two stared at each other.

"I'm no longer employed at the Three Elms," Sam said before Gus had a chance to speak.

The old man nodded, tossing a hasty glance at Emma. "Wouldn't expect you to be."

The caretaker listened patiently while Sam told his mentor what had occurred since he'd been gone.

"David Benton will get what's coming to him," Gus grumbled, when Sam concluded with telling Gus that he and Emma were going to get married. Sam had stepped up behind her, placing his hand on her shoulder. Emma tilted her head to smile up at him.

"I'll be giving Mrs. Benton a piece of my mind," the old man added. "You're the best trainer this place could hope for, and she knows it. One of these days she's going to have to wake up. And if she thinks she can just get rid of you for doing what's right, she's sorely mistaken. I won't stand for this. I will get your job back, or many of us will leave."

Emma's eyes widened at Gus' strong words.

"Don't do anything foolish," Sam said, shaking his head. "Everyone here needs their jobs. And this is your home. Once I'm settled somewhere with Emma, I'll come and get you, if you want. You'll always have a place with me, just like you've given me a place to live."

Gus placed his hand on Sam's arm. "You've been like a son to me, Sam. I know you've told me you've only stayed on because of me." He glanced at Emma. "It's time you thought about your own future. That doesn't mean, however, that I'll just sit by and watch as injustice is done."

Sam smiled at the old man. "Like you said, Benton will get what's coming to him, eventually. At least I won't have to see him ruin this place. Take care of Queen and Dusty for me, will you? Make sure Lonnie doesn't ruin that colt."

Gus shook his head and frowned. "Plum shame what's going to happen to those young horses, with you gone."

Sam nodded. Emma quietly shook her head. Sam and Gus cared about the horses, more than their owners cared for them.

"I'm going to fetch Emma's bags and pack my own gear. I'll only take what I need for now. I'll send for the rest later." He leaned down and kissed Emma's cheek, then told her he'd be back shortly.

Gus walked him to the door. He draped his hand along Sam's shoulder. He leaned toward him, but spoke loud enough for Emma to hear.

"Take the two-seater buggy. Miz Benton won't miss it. If I didn't clean it every week, the wheels would be rusted together by now. You can return it when you're settled."

120

He glanced toward Emma. "Go and get yourself married over in Richmond at the courthouse, then head on over to Ansel Warner's place."

"Ansel Warner?" Sam's brows rose.

"He's got that small farm just a few miles from town. Yesterday, when Millie and I were visiting with the Hobermanns, Ansel mentioned that his trainer was laid up with a kick to the head. He's in Louisville, staying with his sister. Ansel's not sure if he'll ever recover to come back to train. Tell him I sent you."

Sam nodded. He held out his hand to Gus, who shook it. The two embraced. Emma swiped at the tears in her eyes at the scene.

Sam glanced at her one final time, then left the cottage with the promise to be back in a few minutes with her belongings. In the meantime, Gus would hitch up the buggy for them to leave the Three Elms.

Emma paced the floor in the small kitchen. This cottage was a bit larger than the apartment she'd left behind in Lawrence, but it had a warmth to it as if she could feel the years of love and laughter contained within its walls. The large Benton estate with its vast rooms and spacious corridors seemed cold in comparison.

Sam returned with her bag and she changed into the dress she'd worn the day she'd arrived in Lexington. She laughed out loud, standing in Sam's small bedroom, buttoning up the last of the bodice. Never in her wildest dreams had she imagined this would be her wedding dress someday. She glanced at the torn, expensive gown she'd tossed onto the bed, then strode from the room.

Sam waited for her, his eyes meeting hers the instant she walked into the kitchen. Something warm wrapped itself around her heart. Emma took his hand when he held it out to her.

"Ready for your new life, Miss Waterston?" He

leaned forward and kissed her lightly on the lips.

She nodded. "As long as it's with you, Mr. Hawley, I'm ready."

He led her to the door, but it burst open before he could open it himself. Millie swept into the room like a blast of air, her eyes roaming frantically around the space. Spotting Emma, she pulled her into a tight embrace, knocking the wind from Emma's lungs.

"I'm gonna kill that evil man myself," she cried, still clutching Emma tightly to her bosom. "Maybe I'll poison his stew. And for Miz Benton, to do something as foolish as letting Sam go." She held Emma at arm's length away from her, giving Emma a chance to finally take a breath, and frowned with disapproval. "Her horses will never run the same again, mark my word." She nodded, reaffirming her conviction.

"Emma and I are getting married," Sam announced, his voice filled with pride.

No doubt he wanted to steer Millie's anger away from the unpleasant subject of the Bentons. The cook's face instantly shifted from an angry frown to a bright smile. She clasped her hands together, then advanced on Sam and Emma, spreading out her arms. She hugged them both at the same time before finally letting go. Emma took a quick step back. It would take some time for her to get used to this kind of affection.

"And that's the best news I've heard in ages," Millie exclaimed. "Gus already told me. He also said that you're leaving. As soon as you two are settled, we're coming and we're gonna celebrate properly. I'll bake the best wedding cake Fayette County has ever seen."

"That will be lovely." Emma clasped Millie's hand.

The cook beamed at her, then wiped at her eyes. "You two best get going. Gus is waiting with the buggy. We're sure gonna miss you, Sam, but wherever you go, you'll do well. Any owner's gonna be lucky to have you come work for him and train his horses. Benton's going to be sorry soon, you mark my words."

Sam ushered Emma from the cottage before Millie went into another of her tirades. He took the bag from her like he'd done the day he'd met her at the train station. This time, when he helped her into the rig, his hands lingered at her waist, sending a ripple of warmth through Emma at his touch. He smiled up at her when she settled on the seat, adjusting her skirt around her legs. He and Gus embraced a final time, then he hopped onto the seat next to her.

Ollie the groom came rushing up the path, a wide-eyed look of disbelief on his face. Standing in front of one of the barns were at least a dozen grooms.

"Take care of Dusty." Sam reached down from the buggy and shook Ollie's hand. The groom nodded wordlessly. The reality of Sam leaving had apparently not sunk in.

Sam clucked to the horse and snapped the reins over its back. Emma turned to wave at Gus and Millie. The two of them stood together, and Millie leaned into the old man. He wrapped his arm around her shoulders and handed her a handkerchief.

Sam kept the horse at a brisk trot heading down the long lane of the Three Elms. He reached for Emma's hand and squeezed it. They sat in comfortable silence as the buggy took them farther away from the farm and toward their new life together. Emma's heart pounded in her chest. She was getting married today. She'd come to Kentucky as a mail order bride, and today she was going to say her vows to the man of her dreams. Her new dreams.

They passed endless fields dotted with horses, and farms of various sizes. Emma marveled again at the beauty of the countryside. Sam guided the buggy through town when they reached Richmond, and stopped in front of the courthouse. He pulled her into his arms after helping her down from the buggy.

"Ready?" he asked, glancing at the imposing building.

"I've never been more ready," she whispered.

The simple ceremony was over in the blink of an eye. After they said their vows, the justice of the peace made short order of pronouncing them man and wife. Then they signed the certificate, and it was done. She was now Mrs. Sam Hawley.

Sam took her to a small restaurant near the courthouse for a bite to eat, then they were on their way to Ansel Warner's farm. Emma hid her nervousness from her new husband. What if the farm owner didn't have a job for Sam? What if Lizette Benton tried to meddle, and was able to make good on her threat that Sam wouldn't find work in the area?

Her worries were short-lived. Emma stood by while Sam shook hands with Mr. Warner.

"Gus has always spoken highly of you, Hawley. I've mentioned to him that if you were ever looking for a job, to send you to me. Glad he finally did."

"I appreciate the opportunity, Mr. Warner."

The farm owner glanced toward the buggy, where Emma waited. "We can talk formalities tomorrow. I'm sure you and your missus will want to get settled. My former trainer wasn't married, so he lived in a bunk above one of the barns. I do have an empty cottage available. It's furnished, but might need a woman's touch to get it up to snuff."

"I'm sure it'll be fine," Sam assured the eager man.

Ansel Warner seemed genuinely pleased to have Sam as his new trainer. This property wasn't nearly as large or grand as the Three Elms, but in all its modesty, the

Warner Farm looked well-kept.

Sam drove the buggy to the cottage that would be their new home. It looked smaller than the one he'd lived in with Gus. A groom ran up behind them, breathing hard.

"Mr. Warner told me to come and take your horse and buggy, so you can get settled," the youth said.

Sam hopped down from the seat and handed him the reins. "Make sure you rub him down good before you put him up," he instructed, then walked to the other side of the buggy.

"I hope this will be good enough for you." Sam held up his hands to lift Emma from the seat.

She gazed into his worried eyes. "Sam, I lived in a tiny, two-bedroom apartment with three other women for a year. This place will be wonderful, especially because it's ours."

His grin produced the familiar indents in his cheeks that always melted her heart. He reached for their bags and together they walked to the front door of their new home. Sam set the luggage on the ground, and opened the door. Emma peered inside and took a step forward, but Sam's hand on her arm stopped her. Her brows raised in a silent question. Before she had a chance to ask why he wouldn't allow her to enter the cottage, he bent forward and scooped her into his arms. Emma squealed and wrapped her arms around his neck for support.

"Someday, I'll carry you over the threshold to our very own place," he whispered against her neck. "For now, this will have to do." He leaned forward and kissed her. Emma sighed in his arms, gripping tightly to his neck.

Sam set her down in the middle of the small room. She glanced around. It looked to be a sitting area and kitchen combined, with a narrow corridor that led to another room. A couple of chairs surrounded a small,

125

round table, and a rocking chair stood in the corner next to a hearth. The kitchen area contained a wood stove next to a sink with a water pump. Although the two windows in the room let in plenty of light, they were dirty and would need a good washing.

Sam brought in their bags and took them through the other door. He was back a moment later and lit the lantern on the table. Their eyes met.

"I'm afraid my cooking skills might be lacking a bit," Emma said with a quiet smile. "Millie taught me a few things, and I managed to produce a passable meal or two back in Lawrence, but—"

Sam stopped her with a gentle kiss. "Mrs. Hawley, you could serve me saddle leather and I don't think I'd care."

Emma gazed into her husband's sincere eyes. Although she should be furious with Lizette and David Benton, she needed to thank them for all the wealth they'd enabled her to find.

"I love you, Sam Hawley," she whispered. His grin widened.

"I think you'll like the bedroom. It's a bit bigger than the one you slept in last night."

Emma swallowed. Her mouth suddenly went dry. She'd slept in Sam's bed last night, but tonight, they would be sleeping in their own bed, together as husband and wife. He stepped closer until their bodies touched. One hand wound around her waist, drawing her fully up against him, while his other hand caressed her cheek. Emma met his lips when he kissed her again, and she wrapped her arms around his neck.

The momentary apprehension eased, replaced by ripples of desire and longing for more. Sam's gentle kisses and his hands caressing the fabric of her dress no longer seemed enough.

126

He deepened the kiss, then swept her up in his arms, his mouth still on hers. Emma's world spun dizzily as he carried her into the other room. Her heart came alive just like the rest of her, eagerly anticipating what was to come in her husband's arms tonight.

Chapter Sixteen

Emma stirred the vegetables that simmered in her pot for soup stock. She wiped her hands on her apron and inhaled the delicious vapors rising from the stove. It would be many hours yet before the soup would be ready, but Millie had told her to start the stock early in the morning and let it cook all day, so that the flavors would be rich beyond compare by suppertime.

She glanced out the window when a gust of wind rattled the panes. Rain pelted against the freshly polished glass. The clock sitting on the mantle above the hearth chimed ten times. It would be another wet day today.

It had been three weeks since she'd become Sam's wife. A smile passed over her lips. Three of the most wonderful weeks she'd ever spent in her entire life had gone by, and each day promised to be better than the next.

While Sam threw himself into his work and got to know the stable staff and the horses he was in charge of training, Emma had immersed herself in the domestic duties of a common wife. She'd given the cottage a thorough cleaning, washed curtains, tablecloths, and linens, and had experimented with cooking. She'd even sewn a new dress for herself with material Millie had brought to her. The skills she'd learned at the textile mill hadn't been forgotten.

Millie and Gus had visited several times already, and Millie had tutored her as much as she could in culinary skills. News from the Three Elms hadn't been pleasant. David Benton had been nastier than ever with the staff, and his demands with the horses had bordered on unreasonable.

"Dusty came up sore the other day," Gus had

grumbled, eliciting a murderous look from Sam. Emma had reached out to him. Sam loved that horse, and it hurt her to see her husband helpless to do anything for the animal.

"I'm keeping my eye on Lonnie, and I've already told him what a coward he is for putting that colt at risk just because Benton's an ass."

Millie had cuffed Gus across the ears, giving him a stern look for his choice of words. "Even if I agree with you, Gus Ferguson, that's no way to talk in front of us women."

Emma had exchanged a quick glance with Sam, and they'd both held back a smile at the antics of their friends.

Evenings were spent in her husband's arms, either sitting in front of the fire, or even out on the porch as the weather allowed, enjoying each other's company. Their time together usually extended into the bedroom once they both decided it was time for bed. Lying in his arms at night, listening to the wind against the window and the rain on the roof over the last few days, she'd never felt safer or more loved.

"I'm telling you, Gus, the way those two look at each other and carry on when they think I can't see, I know there's going to be a little one for you to bounce on your lap by next spring," Millie had predicted. Emma's face had flamed at the time, but the thought brought a rush of warmth to her belly.

Emma stirred the vegetables a final time, making sure they were all submersed in the water, then sat at the kitchen table. She unfolded several sheets of paper, then began to write.

Dearest friends,

It has been weeks since I last wrote to you, and so much has happened. I'm so happy to hear that you,

Gillian and Willow, are both in the family way. I surely hope that all is well with you, Rose, and that you are settling into your new home in Colorado.

As you've advised, Gillian, I followed my heart and am the richest woman in all of Kentucky for it. While I had my doubts when I first came here, it was the best choice I could have made. My life has changed for the better in so many ways, and I am more in love with my husband each and every day. I don't need a large house, a staff of servants, or fine dresses to be happy. I've come to discover that it's the little things that make for true happiness, and Sam is more that I will ever deserve.

All the best to you all, and I look forward to your next correspondence.

Eternally yours,

Emma Hawley

She copied the letter twice more, then folded and sealed each one. She'd just addressed the letter to Gillian, when the door opened and Sam strode in, bringing with him a blast of cold air. He shook the water from his rain slicker, and peeled it off his shoulders.

"Don't take another step, Sam Hawley, unless you remove your boots," Emma warned sternly as she stood. She moved around the table.

Sam favored her with a wide grin. "Yes, ma'am," he said contritely. He hung up his slicker and stepped out of his boots. He dragged his soaked cap from his head, then pulled her into his arms.

"You're not usually back from the barns this early. It's not even mid-morning," Emma muttered against his lips.

"I had a crazy idea to spend the morning with my lovely bride while we wait for this rain to let up." He winked, grinning at her while holding her flush against him.

Emma's forehead scrunched. "Should you be neglecting your horses like that?"

Sam kissed her again. "The track's too muddy to do any effective training. I don't want to risk a lameness, or worse. I've got the grooms walking some of the flightier colts along the shedrows to get them moving a little, but for today, I can't gallop anyone."

"I love how you're always looking out for the horses, Sam." Emma hugged her husband. "And for me," she added, eliciting a love-filled smile from him. "Is the rain ever going to let up?"

"Rain makes for good grass, which makes for good horses." Sam pulled away from her. "But speaking of you, I have something for you."

He reached into his shirt pocket and produced an envelope. Emma's heart sped up.

"A letter from one of my friends?" she asked eagerly.

"Doesn't look like it. The address is from Boston. Mr. Warner brought it to me. Looks like it's been forwarded a few times."

Emma frowned and reached for the letter. She opened it carefully and unfolded the paper. The familiar handwriting sent her heart racing. She glanced at Sam, then stepped away from him.

"It's from my father," she whispered.

Sam met her gaze. He moved toward the stove and poured himself a cup of coffee from the pot she had warming. No doubt he was simply giving her some space.

Emma scanned the letter and her hand flew to her mouth. She must have gasped, for Sam was beside her in the next instant. He took the paper from her trembling hand, but looked at her rather than reading the letter.

"Everything all right?" he asked, and ran his hand down her arm.

Emma stared up at him. "Sam," she murmured and

131

swallowed. "He's wired twenty-thousand dollars to a bank in Lexington in my name."

"What?" Sam frowned.

"He says one of his business ventures finally paid off, and he's sorry for all the hurt he's caused me and Mother. Apparently he's been trying to find me to give me this money."

Sam's face hardened. "What do you intend to do?"

Emma shook her head. "What do you mean?"

He looked angry.

"What do you plan to do with that kind of money? It's a small fortune."

She stepped up to him and touched her hand to his chest. "It's our money," she said. "We do whatever you and I decide. If you'd rather I didn't accept it, then that's what I'll do."

Sam ran a hand through his hair. He provided for her, but it had occurred to her already that he might be thinking he didn't do enough to keep her happy.

"Sam." She stood on her toes and touched her lips to his. "This changes nothing. I love you. I don't need this money. I need you."

Sam pulled her into an embrace. "I hope I make you happy, Emma, and that you have no regrets about marrying me."

She shook her head and held his face between her hands. "Never," she whispered. "You're all I want. I've never been happier in my life. Maybe I shouldn't accept anything from him, and send it back. If you don't want it, then I don't want it, either."

He shook his head. "No, Emma. You deserve this, and it looks like your father is trying to make amends for what he did to you."

"It can stay in the bank for now," she said quickly. "We can decide later what to do with it."

"I've never accepted money from anyone that I didn't earn myself, Emma. Forgive me for being hesitant." He offered a smile.

"I know," she whispered. "It's for us, though, for our future. I know you've dreamed of your own farm, and breeding your own horses. Here is your chance."

Sam pulled her tightly to him, when someone knocked. Emma moved away from him, letting Sam open the door. Ansel Warner stood outside, water streaming down his hat.

"Hawley, I think you need to come," he said, panting heavily. "I just got word that a tornado touched down a couple miles away. If what I was told is true, it was making a straight line for the Three Elms."

Emma's hand flew to her mouth.

"I'll be right out," Sam said, turning back to her. Ansel nodded and headed back out into the rain.

"What does that mean?" Emma grabbed for his arm, staring at Sam with wide eyes.

"I don't know." The worry on his face was unmistakable.

"I've heard of tornados and the kind of destruction they can cause. You're not planning to go there, are you?"

"I have to make sure Gus is all right." The worried look in his eyes brought a rush of dread racing down her spine.

"Let me come with you," she pleaded. He turned away from her and slipped into his boots.

"Out of the question," he said more forcefully than he'd ever spoken to her. He slipped into his wet rain slicker.

"Sam, be careful."

Emma grabbed for his arms. She stared up at him. He leaned down and kissed her gently.

"I will be. I won't do anything foolish, I promise, but

I have to find out about Gus and Millie."

She nodded. What else could she do? She loved Gus, too, and prayed that he was safe.

"When will you be back?"

"Hopefully by nightfall." He set his cap on his head, then opened the door.

Emma hugged her shawl around her shoulders, and shivered. Sam splashed through the mud toward the barns. She stood in the doorway and didn't close the door until the horse he rode off on disappeared in the rain.

Inside the warmth and security of the cottage, she leaned heavily against the door. Her hands were numb from the cold, but so was her heart. What if something happened to him?

"You're my world, Sam. Please be safe," she whispered.

The hours dragged on. Morning turned to afternoon, then to evening. The rain had let up sometime around suppertime, but the soup sat cold and forgotten on the stove. Emma lit a lamp and sat in the rocking chair by the hearth. Her eyes burned from crying all day, and fell on the discarded letter from her father. It must have fallen to the ground at some point.

Emma didn't bother picking it up. She didn't care about the money. Sam's near-angry face haunted her as the conversation replayed in her mind of when she'd told him what her father had gifted her. Would the issue of money always hang between them? Hopefully she'd proven to Sam that he was more important to her than all the riches in the world.

A loud bang, followed by a gust of wind, startled her from a restless sleep in the rocking chair. She opened her eyes and winced at the pain in her stiff neck. When had she dozed off? The room was dim, lit only by the soft glow of the lantern. One look toward the door and she bolted to her feet.

"Sam?"

Emma threw herself at her husband. He was drenched, cold, and muddy. It didn't matter. He wrapped his arms around her, pulling her into a fierce embrace.

"Are you all right?" she cried against his damp neck, water dripping onto her cheeks from his hair.

"I'm fine," he murmured against her face. "Everything is fine."

"I was so worried about you," she cried.

Sam set her away from him, then slipped out of his wet clothes. Emma hurried to stoke the fire in the hearth.

"It'll take me a minute to get the fire going in the stove so I can heat up some soup and get some coffee brewing. You're frozen to the bone."

The clock on the mantle chimed twice. It was two o'clock in the morning?

Sam looked tired and haggard. Wordlessly, he slipped into their bedroom and changed into dry clothes. When he returned, Emma held out a mug with coffee.

"Thank you," he said and wrapped his hands around the hot mug.

He sat at the table. Emma joined him and waited.

"The Three Elms is in ruin," he finally said. He raised his head to look at her from across the table. "Most of the barns are destroyed, and all the outbuildings. Fences are down, and it'll take them days to round up all the horses that got loose."

"Gus? Millie?" Emma croaked.

"They're fine. They were able to take shelter with the others in the storm cellar. The estate is damaged, but it's still standing. David Benton is missing."

Emma's hand flew to her mouth. "Missing?"

"No one knows where he went. Mrs. Benton is beside herself. It was too dark to continue searching for him."

Emma nodded. As ruthless as David was, she didn't wish this on him, or anyone.

Sam took a sip of his coffee, then stared at her. When he reached his hand out she grabbed it. He squeezed hers tightly.

"I found Dusty," he said slowly. "He was caught up between some downed trees. His legs are pretty bad."

"Sam," Emma whispered. Her hold on his hand tightened.

"Gus told me he was already lame. Apparently, Lonnie worked him over a wet track the other day, and he wasn't completely sound to begin with. He slipped in the mud and fell."

Sam visibly clenched his jaw. "I made Lizette Benton an offer on him. She sold him to me for two thousand dollars, after I convinced her I had the money. She figured he was worthless anyway, being lame, so she agreed, as long as I bring her the money tomorrow." His stare from across the table intensified. "I'm sorry, Emma. I couldn't leave him there. I'm sorry I spent your money."

Emma sprang from her seat and crossed to his side of the table. She leaned down and wrapped her arms around her husband.

"I would have been upset with you, Sam Hawley, if you hadn't bought that horse," she said in a stern voice. "Even if he'll never run again. But knowing you, you'll bring him back, and he'll be the champion you know he can be."

Sam stood, then pulled her into his arms. "I've never spent money I didn't have."

She shook her head. "It's your money, Sam. Ours. We're in this together. Just as I'm growing fond of not having money, perhaps you should grow fond of the fact that you had the means to save this horse."

She stared up at him, willing him to understand and

see her side. "Dusty and his dam, if you want to buy her, too, will be the start of the finest racing and breeding establishment this state has ever seen."

Emma smiled through her tears.

"Are you sure that's what you want?" Sam's hold around her tightened.

She wrapped her arms around his neck and pulled his face closer to hers, kissing him with all the love in her heart. After today, he would never doubt her again.

"I love you, Sam Hawley. I'm your Bride of Kentucky. Of course it's what I want."

Epilogue

One Year Later...

"Congratulations, Cousin."

Sam accepted a hearty handshake from his cousin, Trace, then he turned and pulled Emma into a tight embrace.

"Looks like the Derby is becoming a family tradition," she beamed, smiling from him to Trace. "I'm so glad you could be here to celebrate with us."

Trace Hawley grinned. "I just wish I had brought Katie. She would have loved to meet you, but she has her hands full at home with the little ones. It's just a stroke of luck that I came to Kentucky, looking for some mares to buy. I had no idea that my little cousin had a horse entered in the Derby."

"Maybe we'll make it up to Montana someday and take a look at the kind of horses you're breeding up there." Sam winked at his cousin.

"My horses will give your bluebloods a run for their money any day," Trace shot back. "But I will say, I doubt any horse could have beaten Dusty today."

"He's always been a champion, but Sam's the one who trained him how to run." Emma wrapped her arms more fully around his neck, and Sam kissed her in front of the crowd of well-wishers that surrounded them.

"I'm personally looking forward to getting back to your place," Trace said with a grin. "I've enjoyed Millie's cooking over the last few days. I heard win or lose, she was putting on quite a spread for tonight."

"If she has her way, no one's going to leave the farm with any complaints of not getting enough to eat."

Sam set Emma down, but held tight to her hand. With Trace leading the way to make room for them to get through the crowd, they headed for the winner's circle. Together, he and Emma accepted the winner's trophy, and she was presented with a large bouquet of red roses.

"Someone should make a blanket of roses for the winning horse," she whispered to Sam. "I certainly don't deserve these. Dusty did all the work."

"Maybe you can suggest it, and it'll become tradition someday." Sam winked at her.

Holding her hand, he led Dusty out of the winner's circle and back to the barns. Trace stopped to talk to someone who remembered him from several years ago, when he'd been in the winner's circle with his Montana-bred Derby winner.

Sam handed the colt over to his groom. He pulled Emma aside and held her tight. "Have I told you lately that I'm the luckiest man in the state of Kentucky?"

Emma smiled up at him. Unlike the other fine ladies who attended the races, and this race in particular, she'd chosen not to wear a stylish hat. In fact, her plain, home-sewn clothes had been frowned upon by the Kentucky elite.

"You're going to get all the ladies talking, Mrs. Hawley, that I don't provide for my wife."

"You provide for me just fine," she whispered, and leaned in for a kiss. "The fine ladies of the establishment have no idea how well you provide for me."

Sam's insides heated. He'd never get tired of his wife's teasing. In the year since they'd married, he'd become more accepting of having some money to spend, which had all gone back into the horses. Not once had she ever complained that she didn't own the latest fashions or that she lacked in other amenities.

After the devastation of the tornado, Sam had managed to purchase a small farm with the money Emma's father had given her. She'd insisted on it, and had worked right alongside him to rebuild the damaged barns, pastures, and the modest house. They'd both agreed that their venture would always remain small, and they'd only keep enough animals that they could comfortably manage.

Gus and Millie had finally tied the knot, and now lived on Sam and Emma's property. Gus managed the business end of the operation, while Millie continued to teach Emma the fineries of cooking.

Although she hadn't seen her father, Emma had been corresponding with him over the last year. She didn't talk about him too much, and although she hadn't completely forgiven him about what he'd done to her and her mother, at least they were keeping in touch.

David Benton had never been found. Speculation was that he'd been caught in the tornado and his body had been swept away by the forces of nature. Lizette Benton hadn't recovered from the loss of her son and the ruin of her estate. She'd become a recluse, and no one ever saw her.

"Our racing barn is well on its way, Mrs. Hawley, and with Dusty, we'll start a nice little breeding farm, too."

"That's not the only breeding operation that's well underway." She blushed visibly.

Sam's brows furrowed. He stared at her, then he smiled broadly and lifted her in a tight embrace.

"I love you, Emma Hawley."

"And I love you, Sam Hawley. I can't believe that a year ago I came to Kentucky without a penny to my name, and now I'm the richest woman in the entire state."

If you enjoyed reading this book, there are 49 more in the series! Find out about the rest of the American Mail-Order   Brides   here http://www.newwesternromance.com

To specifically read about Willow, Rose, and Gillian, Emma's friends, their stories can be found under the following titles:

Willow, Bride of Pennsylvania

Rose, Bride of Colorado

Gillian, Bride of Maine

Dear Reader

I hope you enjoyed reading Emma, Bride of Kentucky (Book 15 in the American Mail-Order Brides Series) as much as I enjoyed writing it. While my usual setting for my romances is the wilds of the Montana and Wyoming Rockies, I've had fun writing a romance set somewhere slightly different.

I write about mountain men and fur trappers, and the women who were brave enough to forge a life in the harsh wilderness of the 1800's before the area - what is today considered the Greater Yellowstone Area - was settled. I've also taken my characters on adventures along the Oregon Trail, and enjoy settings on Montana ranches, with rugged cowboys.

I couldn't resist bringing a character from one of my other books into Emma's story for a very minor role. To read Trace Hawley's story, it is the first in my Blemished Brides Series, called IN HIS EYES.

My readers will also find one or two other "easter eggs" in this book.

When I was first asked to join in this 50-book project, I was hoping to get Montana or Wyoming as my state for my bride, but those were already snatched up. I picked Kentucky, because I used to be a big horseracing fan as a teenager and in my early twenties. I used to dream of owning my own beautiful thoroughbred farm in Bluegrass Country before I discovered Yellowstone. My first horse was an off-track thoroughbred, and I've since owned and retrained several former racehorses.

I no longer follow the sport as much as I used to, but there are few things more exhilarating or beautiful than watching horses run through green pastures.

Kentucky has been a major state for horse breeding and racing, tracing its traditions back to the late 18th century. The Bluegrass Region has always been noted as an area producing superior racehorses, due to the mineral content in the soil.

The Kentucky Derby is one of the most famous horse races in the world, and takes place on the first Saturday in May at Churchill Downs in Louisville, Kentucky. The first Kentucky Derby race was held on May 17, 1875 in front of a crowd of 10,000 people.

The Derby was dubbed "The Run for the Roses" in 1925 by a New York Sports columnist because a blanket of 554 roses is draped over the Derby winner in the winner's circle each year. This tradition is thought to have started when roses were presented to the ladies at a post-Derby party in 1883. The roses created such a sensation with the ladies that the track president decided to feature the rose as the official flower for the 1884 Kentucky Derby. The first account of roses actually draped over the winning horse came in 1896.

As always, my thanks goes out to my editor, Barbara Ouradnik, and my cover designer, Collin Henderson.

Other Books by Peggy L Henderson

Blemished Brides Western Historical Romance:
In His Eyes
In His Touch
In His Arms

Yellowstone Romance Series:
(in recommended reading order)

Yellowstone Heart Song
A Yellowstone Christmas (novella)
Yellowstone Redemption
Yellowstone Homecoming (novella)
Yellowstone Awakening
Yellowstone Dawn
A Yellowstone Season of Giving (short Story)
Yellowstone Deception
A Yellowstone Promise (novella)
Yellowstone Origins

Second Chances Time Travel Romance Series

Come Home to Me
Ain't No Angel
Diamond in the Dust

Teton Romance Trilogy
Teton Sunrise
Teton Splendor
Teton Sunset
Teton Season of Joy (novella)

Find out more about me and my stories here:

www.peggylhenderson.com

Join me on Facebook. I love interacting with my readers, and you can stay current on my book projects and happenings.

I'm always happy to hear from my readers. Tell me what you liked, or didn't like in the story. I can be reached via email here:

vmpdreamer@gmail.com

CPSIA information can be obtained
at www.ICGtesting.com
Printed in the USA
FFOW02n0729080116
20246FF